USA TODAY bestse
is a voracious reade
author her whole lif
Lit subjects into her
she got a job in corp
wasn't long before sh
After leaving her hometown of Melbourne to start a
new adventure in Toronto, she now spends her days
writing contemporary romances with humour, heat
and heart.

For more information on Stefanie and her books
check out her website at stefanie-london.com
or her Facebook page at Facebook.com/
stefanielondonauthor.

If you liked *Unmasked*, why not try

Her Dirty Little Secret by JC Harroway
The Marriage Clause by Alexx Andria
Inked by Anne Marsh

Discover more at millsandboon.co.uk

UNMASKED

STEFANIE LONDON

MILLS & BOON

First Published in Great Britain 2018
by Mills & Boon, an imprint of HarperCollins*Publishers*
1 London Bridge Street, London, SE1 9GF

© 2018 Stefanie Little

ISBN: 978-0-263-93213-3

MIX
Paper from
responsible sources
FSC® C007454

This book is produced from independently certified FSC™ paper
to ensure responsible forest management.
For more information visit www.harpercollins.co.uk/green.

Printed and bound in Spain
by CPI, Barcelona

To Canada, thanks for letting me stay.

CHAPTER ONE

LAINEY KLINE STARED at the chocolate cake, which had the words *sorry I'm leaving you* piped in shaky white icing. Was an apology dessert over the top? Subtlety had never been her style, and announcing that she had secured a new job—and planned to relocate from Melbourne to London—required a special touch. A special *chocolate* touch.

Her two best friends, Imogen and Corinna, stared at her. "You're breaking up with us via cake?" Imogen said. "Seriously?"

"This isn't a breakup," Lainey replied, trying her hardest to replicate the positive spiel she'd practised in front of her mirror. "I'm simply suggesting a long-distance relationship."

Imogen shook her head. "A month is *not* enough time to say goodbye."

"I can't believe you kept it quiet for a whole week." Corinna grinned.

The three of them sat at the picnic table in Corinna's parents' backyard. Even though Corinna had moved out two years ago, the three women still loved to congregate at the McKnight family home, especially during the summer. Their lush, sprawling garden was filled with native trees that attracted colourful birds like rosellas and galahs. Their song usually soothed Lainey, but not today.

"It wasn't easy, believe me." Lainey watched the bubbles race to the top of her champagne flute. "When I booked the flight, I wanted to scream it from the rooftops. But I had to tell you both at once, and you two are so difficult to coordinate."

Between Imogen's long hours and Corinna's bustling social schedule, it'd taken a week to find a day where they were both free. But that was their deal— all news had to be shared as a group. Easier to avoid the whole "three's a crowd" issue if there were no favourites. But it wouldn't be like that for much longer. Worry stabbed Lainey in the gut. She knew her best friends would grow closer once she left; hopefully they wouldn't forget about her altogether.

Hence the cake. Hard to forget about a person who piped her apologies in buttercream.

"So, hairdresser to the stars, huh? Maybe you'll end up doing the royal family." Imogen forced a smile, but her eyes glimmered with moisture. "Well, Prince Harry, anyway. Poor old Wills hasn't got much left. He's already in comb-over territory."

"I doubt they'll let me near the royals," Lainey said, reaching for the big knife next to the cake and slicing straight through *sorry*. "Besides, I'll be more focused on the social media side of things."

Lainey had been a hairdresser ever since she

walked out of school on her sixteenth birthday. Now she had eight years in the industry, which was by far the longest time she'd ever stuck to anything. Certainly longer than her failed attempts at reading tarot cards or working as a Red Bull promo girl. Two years ago, bored and desperate for creativity, she'd started posting her hairstyles on Instagram. Within a year, she'd amassed over a million followers and had brands foaming at the mouth to work with her.

Then she'd parlayed that into a gig as a social media consultant with a well-known celebrity hairstylist in London.

"But the contract is only six months, right?" Imogen asked as she handed a slice of cake to Corinna. "Then you'll come back?"

"I'm hoping they'll put me on permanently." The finality of the move settled in the pit of Lainey's stomach.

"Of course we'll miss you," Corinna said, shooting Imogen a look, "but I'm glad you've found a way to turn your passion into a job. This sounds like an amazing opportunity."

With the scent of eucalyptus on the breeze and the late-afternoon sun beating down, Lainey wondered if she should have picked another location for her big announcement. There were so many memories here. And, as excited as she was about her new job, the thought of leaving her best friends behind made her feel ill. Like her body physically rejected the idea of them being apart.

It's for the best. You've been miserable, and a fresh start is exactly *what you need.*

"I'm happy for you, too," Imogen said, her words a little blurred around the edges. The girl was a total lightweight—two champagnes and she was already entering tipsyville. "But I *do* wish you'd been able to find such a cool job here."

"I need to get away." Much to her horror, Lainey's voice wobbled.

Imogen frowned. "Get away from what?"

A confession hovered on the tip of her tongue. She wanted to blurt her secret, but what was the point? The decision was made. She was leaving in one short month, and Lainey made it a rule not to dwell on the negative.

"I just meant there are more opportunities overseas," she said carefully. "I'm going nowhere here. Marsha didn't seem to care that I resigned, since she thinks we're all replaceable, and it's not like I have a relationship to tie me down. Thank *God*."

She hoped the booze would prevent Imogen from noticing how false Lainey's voice sounded. Corinna raised a brow but mercifully didn't press for more information.

"But you're sworn to secrecy," Lainey went on. "I want to tell everyone else myself." She looked them both in the eye and smiled when they nodded. "I'd rather people hear it directly from me."

Although the interview process for this job had been going on for almost two months, Lainey hadn't breathed a word of it to anyone until she'd signed a contract and booked her flight a week ago. Part of her hadn't really believed it would happen. Even now, the whole thing felt a little surreal.

"Have you got a 'before I leave the motherland' bucket list?" Corinna asked. "There must be something you want to do before you go."

Not something, but some*one*. Lainey's move was as much about chasing her career dreams as it was about escaping the futility of her situation in Melbourne. She'd done something dumb. Idiotic. Monumentally stupid.

An action that might one day be documented in her memoir, under the title "Ways I Like to Torture Myself."

Over the years, Lainey had developed a gigantic crush on the one guy who was totally and utterly out of reach. The one guy who wouldn't look twice at her—Corinna's big brother.

Worse, seeing Damian McKnight get married, divorced and then pimped out on *Australia's Most Eligible* had torn her up inside. All her dreams for turning her adoration of rom-coms into a romantic reality had vanished. The only solution was to be somewhere else, so she could focus on the important stuff—like her career—and forget that she was doomed to have a miserable love life because she wanted the one man she couldn't have.

"This is the perfect opportunity to go wild," Corinna said. "You can do whatever you like here, then flit off to England without consequences. Surely there's someone you've always wished you could have it out with. Maybe a crazy customer that you hate?"

"Or maybe I should tell your brother I think he's hot," Lainey said with a wink. Corinna pretended to stick her fingers down her throat, and the three women laughed.

It was a running gag—both Lainey and Imogen considered Damian McKnight to be the highest level of hotness—usually reserved for the Hemsworth brothers and Prince Harry. But jokes were the only thing keeping Lainey's deep-seated attraction a secret—because the more she overplayed it, the less they believed it was anything serious. Therefore, she could hide in plain sight.

He was her Prince Charming, her Mr. Darcy, the Harry to her Sally. The Danny to her Sandra Dee. The only guy who'd ever truly known her.

"Speaking of Damian," Corinna said, "did you know he scored a ticket to the Carmina Ball?"

"Wow." Imogen blinked. "My sister's stupid fiancé is going…without her, I might add, which has shocked absolutely no one."

The Carmina Ball was something Lainey only knew about from drooling over red carpet dresses online. It was invite only and distinctly too upper-crust for lowly hairdressers like her.

"Apparently it's five grand to attend," Imogen added. "Five. Freaking. Grand!"

"I bet that's a drop in the ocean to them," Lainey said, rolling her eyes. "But still, Damian must be excited he scored an invite."

"Who knows with him?" Corinna shrugged. "That guy seems to have a permanent scowl on his face these days. I told him to be careful—the wind might change and then he'll be stuck with that ugly mug for the rest of his life."

Lainey snorted. "I'd still do him."

Imogen almost choked on her cake as Corinna visibly shuddered and said, "You guys are disgusting."

"He's cute, Cori. I know you're related, but you have to admit it." Imogen grinned.

"We are *not* talking about my brother," Corinna said. "Besides, I want to know what the gossip is with your sister, Immie. You're telling me Richie Rich couldn't afford to get her a ticket?"

"He said that it's going to be all business and that he'd rather spend the money to take her on a romantic getaway to some fancy-pants resort in Thailand than get her a ticket to the ball." Imogen's lips curled back into an uncharacteristic sneer. "But *I* think it's because he's cheating on her with someone who'll be there."

"Whoa." Lainey held up her hands. "Since when is he cheating on her?"

"Penny said something that has been bothering me for ages. Dan goes to Sydney a few days each month for work." Imogen toyed with her pearl earring. "Last month I was at the Boatbuilders Yard in South Wharf having drinks with people from work, and I saw him."

"But he was supposed to be in Sydney?" Corinna asked.

"Yep, and I'd spoken to Penny that afternoon. She said he wasn't coming back until the following night." She gritted her teeth. "I didn't know what to do. He was with this blonde and they looked like they were flirting, but I lost him in the crowd."

"Did you tell Penny?" Lainey asked.

Imogen sighed. "I tried to, but she accused me of hating him from day one. She wouldn't listen."

"Perhaps he came home early," Lainey suggested. "He might've been called back for a meeting. It could be completely innocent."

"I can't explain it…" Imogen sighed. "I know something is going on. I'm *sure* of it."

"What are you going to do?" Lainey asked.

Imogen fished her phone out of her pocket and pulled up a photo of a woman wearing a mask. It was covered in pink stones, the colour of rosé. White feathers sprayed up from the top, and lengths of superfine chain in rose gold hung down in elegant loops on either side.

"Is that you?" Lainey asked, and Imogen nodded. "I'm not following."

"I'm going to sneak into the Carmina Ball. Then I'm going to catch him in the act and make sure my sister doesn't walk down the aisle with the wrong guy."

Lainey squinted at the picture, the intricate design of the gems and beads mesmerising her. It was impossible to see Imogen's features. Add some dramatic makeup and a wig or change of hair colour, and her identity would truly be concealed.

"You're crazy," Corinna said with a shake of her head. Her phone buzzed and she snatched it off the table. "Sorry, ladies, it's Joe. I need to take this."

"Hi, Joe!" Lainey and Imogen chorused when she answered the phone, dissolving into laughter when Corinna rolled her eyes and headed into the house.

"Where's the loyalty?" Imogen said as she reached for her champagne and sloshed a little over the edge. They were *definitely* getting an Uber home tonight.

"He does seem like a decent guy," Lainey said. "She has better luck than me, that's for damn sure. I haven't been on a date in months."

Imogen laughed. "That means your life hasn't been unnecessarily complicated for months."

"I thought you enjoyed hearing about my dating disasters." Lainey grinned and scooped some icing off what was left of the cake. Her message was now an incoherent mess. "Solid entertainment value there."

Disasters was certainly the right word. While Corinna always attracted cute, decent men, Lainey ended up in every kind of impossible, couldn't-make-it-up dating scenario there was. She'd dated a guy who turned out to be as old as her father, two ex-cons and a circus performer who liked to watch her walk around wearing only a pair of mismatched socks.

"In a kind of masochistic way…yeah, I do." Imogen forked some cake into her mouth.

"Why is it masochistic?"

"Because I know I'll be picking up the pieces when it goes bad." Imogen's eyes sparkled as an amused smile formed. "What happened when that guy wanted

you to move to the hippie commune in Nimben? I told
you not to go with him."

"I didn't go with him...well, not all the way."
Lainey bit down on her lip to stifle a laugh.

Okay, so Imogen was usually the voice of reason.
Which made her plans to sneak into the Carmina Ball
all the more interesting. The thing was, if anyone was
going to break the rules and do it properly, it would
be Imogen. She'd have plans and contingencies and
all the necessary details worked out.

"I drove all the way to the state border to drag
your butt home," Imogen said, crossing her arms.
"And what about the time you decided to go camp-
ing in the middle of nowhere with that guy who got
arrested and left you stranded?"

"I didn't know the car was stolen." Lainey shrugged.
"Besides, I'm pretty sure Damian bailed me out that
particular occasion."

Imogen chuckled. "Speak of the devil."

Lainey's head whipped around. The object of her
fantasies was in the doorway. Damian McKnight, in
all his panty-singeing glory, wearing a pair of faded
blue jeans that hugged his thighs to perfection. His
blue checked shirt was open at the collar and rolled
back at the sleeves, inviting Lainey's eyes to linger
on smooth olive skin.

"What were you saying about me?" he asked warily
as he walked over.

As usual, Lainey gave him a saccharine smile,
which he didn't return. He might have been all biceps
and close-up-worthy eyes, but Damian McKnight was

the sworn enemy of all that was fun. Mr. Stick Up His Butt, she'd called him once.

It was truly baffling why she found his serious-ness so damn appealing.

He used to be fun before Jenny broke his heart into a million little pieces. Maybe you need to show him how to have fun again...

Yeah, right. Damian had always acted like she was a little bug that buzzed around him, invading his space. Hanging around where she wasn't wanted. And the one time she'd gotten drunk and tried to kiss him the year after he got divorced, he'd made it clear he wouldn't go there with her, despite the fact that he'd been giving her eyes all night. She was twenty-one then, and fully aware of what she wanted with him.

"We were reminiscing about some of Lainey's finer dating moments," Imogen said.

Damian smirked. "Like that time you had to climb out that lawyer's window because his other girlfriend came home early?"

"He told me he was single," Lainey protested, reaching for her drink. "I would *never* have dated him if I'd known."

He shook his head. He often did that around her... they *all* did. "Where's your third musketeer?"

"Inside, talking to her lover boy," Lainey replied.

"And what about you?" His gaze skated over her. "Any recent victims?"

Lainey drained the rest of her champagne and tried to appear as though she hadn't noticed the searing look. Damian had the Blue Steel thing down pat, and she knew for a fact that women all over Melbourne would give their right arm to be on the receiving end of it. And since his stint on TV, the guy even had a fan club on Facebook. A freaking fan club!

"I love being single, you know that. But I might head out later, see if anyone takes my interest."

His jaw tensed. *Interesting*. "If you do, be sure to give him my condolences."

There was a strange undercurrent in Damian's tone, a little hum of tension that sent ripples of curiosity through her. Was it because he didn't care or because he didn't like the idea of her chatting someone up?

She never could tell with him. He said he wasn't interested, but his body language told a different story.

"And what are you up to tonight?" she asked.

"Not much. Mum needed a hand with the pipes in the kitchen, and Dad's back is still giving him a hard time," he said with a brisk nod. "I'm exchanging hard labour for lasagne."

Well, damn if that didn't make her insides melt. Despite his sharp rise in business and wealth, Damian never forgot where he came from or who was important in his life. He was dedicated to his family, always making himself available for his parents or his sister.

It still baffled Lainey why his wife had left. Who in their right mind would walk away from *him*?

Damian's eyes flicked over her once more, and she felt it all the way down to her toes. "Anyway, I'd better get to it. Behave yourselves, okay?"

"Never." Lainey had to contain a laugh as he rolled his eyes, walking away without a backward glance.

The man had an ass so perfect it should be in a gallery.

"So uptight," Lainey muttered, her eyes locked onto the way his hips rolled as he disappeared into the house. "But so *smoking* hot."

Imogen snorted. "I think you mean 'so unattainable.'"

"Potato, po-*tah*-to." Lainey tapped her nails against the table. "So, I want to know more about this whole Carmina Ball plan. I'm intrigued."

"I was going to keep it a secret." Imogen dropped her face into her hands. "But Corinna kept topping up my glass and then with the shock of your news, I...ugh. Please don't tell anyone."

"My lips are sealed." Lainey mimicked turning a key in a lock. "How are you going to get in without an invitation?"

"I know the caterer." Imogen leaned forward. "I'll arrive with her team and then slip off to change into my costume after the party starts."

Lainey sucked on her lower lip. The plan was totally insane. Absolutely and utterly bonkers.

Speaking of Damian, did you know he scored a ticket to the Carmina Ball?

Corinna's words rang in her head like a siren song, along with the teasing thought of being able to do anything she wanted before leaving for London. If Imogen could sneak into the ball in disguise, Lainey could, too.

What the hell will you do once you get in?

Anything. A wicked smile curved on her lips. She could do anything at all.

"I don't suppose there's room for a sidekick on this grand adventure?" Lainey asked.

"Now why would you want to do that?"

While Lainey was confident in her seduction abilities with men in general, Damian seemed to be her white whale. He resisted her where other men didn't, and she had her suspicions it wasn't due to a lack of physical chemistry. They had it in excess. Her body sparked whenever he came near her. And as for him... well, she'd caught him looking at her before with that heated blue gaze. But for some reason, he never acted on her flirty suggestions, never returned any teasing innuendo.

But the whole point of a masquerade ball was to have a little fun without revealing your identity, right? She could test her theory that they did have something between them.

Damian McKnight had a hold over her unlike anyone else. He was a man among boys. A total and utter fantasy.

In quiet moments, she'd wondered if he was the reason she chose to date flighty, flaky types. She could never have Damian, so she went for the opposite—the loose cannons and the jokers. The guys who would never tempt her into falling in love.

"Let me revise that," Imogen said, narrowing her eyes. "Do I *want* to know?"

"Probably not," Lainey admitted. Her eyes snagged

on the empty doorway where Damian had exited a few minutes ago.

"Are you doing what I think you're doing?" Imogen asked, tracking Lainey's gaze. "Not a good idea."

"Please, Immie," she said. "He won't know it's me. I'll keep my mask on and I'll get out of there if things go bad."

"I thought you were only trying to wind Corinna up." Her friend gripped her drink, her hand hovering in midair as though she'd forgotten about it. "Were you serious about him this whole time?"

"I was," she admitted. "But he never treated me as anything more than a little sister type. Please. This might be my only chance. Once I'm gone…that's it."

After a moment, Imogen threw her hands in the air. "Fine. But I will not take sides if this blows up."

Lainey bit her lip, trying to trap the excitement inside her. One night to see if her fantasies could come true. Then she'd move on and pretend it never happened.

CHAPTER TWO

DAMIAN'S WEEK HAD started bad and ended in a steaming pile of crap. Seeing Lainey over the weekend had distracted him with all kinds of inappropriate thoughts, which made him guilty and snappy. He was like Snow White's rejected eighth dwarf.

Distraction he could handle. Failure, on the other hand…that was *not* tolerable.

"How'd the meeting go?" Aaron reached for his gin and tonic. They'd arranged to meet at their usual place, an older bar that was no longer trendy, which therefore meant you could get decent service. Plus, with the Carmina Ball happening tomorrow night, Damian was sure he'd need to store up all his energy. Parties weren't really his thing, but getting an invite was akin to being accepted by people who mattered. And while everyone would be in masquerade dress, he'd been told a lot of business was conducted if you knew the right people and asked the right questions.

It all sounded a little secret society to him.

He grunted. "Don't ask."

"That good, huh?"

Damian tossed back his drink, trying to drown the sick feeling in his stomach. Tonight's meeting was supposed to have been the start of a new era for his management consulting business. Another rung climbed toward the shining carrot dangling a hair-breadth out of reach. Validation. Retribution.

Instead he'd gotten a big fat face-to-face rejection. In under five minutes, which was salt in the wound. Not that Damian had ever been frightened of the word *no*. People had knocked him back left, right and cen-tre when he'd first struck out on his own. But this cli-ent was different.

This client was personal.

"He said he didn't want to have his family-friendly image associated with someone like me. Like I'm a fucking social pariah. It was one reality show, for Chrissakes."

He regretted going on *Australia's Most Eligible* more than any other cock-up he'd ever made in his career. He hadn't been looking for love, like the show proclaimed—none of the contestants were. They wanted publicity. Name recognition. At the time, his PR person had assured him it would bring his fledg-ling Melbourne-based business to a national level... and it had. Damian had come across well on-screen, and his business had seen a hearty boost in attention after the show aired.

But mostly it was small stuff. And Damian wasn't happy with bread crumbs—he wanted the whole damn loaf.

Only hard work had allowed him to take his business to the next level. He'd put in long hours and hustled to get clients. Now he was operating at a level most people could only aspire to, but his reality TV show days still hung around like a bad smell.

"And the damn thing is scripted. They turn you into a character—everyone knows that." Damian shook his head. "But he said people who used 'cheap tricks' to get ahead were not the kind of people he wants to do business with. Oh, and apparently those kinds of shows are the reason our society is falling to pieces. Because nobody has 'good, old-fashioned values' anymore."

"He sounds like a dick. Anyway, you always land on your feet," Aaron replied with a shrug. "You'll get another client."

"Of course I will. But I want this one." He turned the empty whisky glass over in his hands. "I just need to figure out how to look more family friendly."

"You?" Aaron laughed. "No offence, mate, but you're not exactly the family-friendly type."

Irritation prickled under Damian's skin. He *knew* that. Getting divorced six months before he turned thirty had put a sour taste in his mouth when it came to families. And relationships. Which meant he dated with an immovable expiry. It worked for him, kept things mess-free, but after his TV stint, more people took notice of his dating habits. Potential clients included.

"What company is it?" Aaron asked.

"McPartlin & Co."

The company had started out with a single restaurant and now owned seven fine dining establishments across the country, plus another recently launched in New Zealand. The owner had also signed a lucrative deal with Coles supermarkets. They even had plans for expansion into Singapore, Hong Kong and Dubai, all within the next five years.

But the owner of the company was notoriously uptight and traditional. Hell, he'd fired one of the best chefs in the world for swearing in the kitchen, because "foul language" shouldn't be tolerated. Given it wasn't unusual for chefs to have a colourful vernacular, the news had made headlines.

"Jerry McPartlin's company." Realisation seeped into Aaron's features. "Your old boss's client?"

"That would be the one."

"Okay, buddy. You need to take a breath and think about this." Aaron put his drink down and planted a hand on Damian's shoulder. "I know you're pissed about what happened, but—"

"He was screwing my wife, Aaron."

That was what this was about. Revenge. The McPartlin & Co. deal had launched Ben's boutique consulting firm into the big leagues. They were his flagship client.

And Damian was going to do everything in his power to take the business from him, the way Ben had taken something precious from Damian.

The memory made red flash before his eyes like a matador's cape. "Then he had the audacity to tell me I'd never make it. That I'd never even come close to playing at his level."

"He's a prick, that's a fact well established." Aaron shook his head. "But you need to let it go. It was four years ago. It's not healthy to hang on to this shit for so long."

"Are you done, Oprah?"

"Sticks and stones, mate. I'm only saying this because you're like a brother to me." He sighed. "Have a few drinks, find a woman and forget about Ben. Forget about Jenny while you're at it. They're not worth the energy."

Aaron was the only person outside his family who knew what'd happened with his divorce and his abrupt departure from Ben's firm. Trust wasn't something Damian had in large supply, especially these days, but he'd put his life in Aaron's hands if the situation called for it.

However, the guy had married his teenage sweetheart and lived a life of sunshine and roses. He didn't understand Damian's need to settle the score.

"Having a few drinks and finding a woman is exactly why McPartlin & Co. thinks I'm wrong for them. I need a change of image."

"And how are you going to do that?"

"Maybe I should get engaged. That'll make me look like family material." Damian drummed his fingers on the bar, his mind whirring. Searching for a solution. "I could be the guy who finally settled down for the right woman."

Aaron looked at him like he was crazy. "And who would you get engaged to?"

"Someone I don't care about." In other words, someone who wouldn't be able to screw him over.

"I'd always assumed if I was going to be in a barn naked, there'd at least be a sexy cowboy involved." Lainey shimmied on the spot, pulling the dress over her hips. It was a touch too tight, but it was a loaner, so she'd have to make do.

"Are you saying I'm not good enough for a roll in the hay?" Imogen grinned. "Now, quit complaining and zip me up."

Both dresses had come from a friend of Imogen's who owned a boutique in Malvern. The sizing options for borrowed dresses had been limited. But since Lainey couldn't afford to shell out a few thousand dollars for a fancy dress, she had to suck in her stomach and avoid eating. One, because the boning in the bodice wouldn't allow for any expansion, and two, because the dresses could not get dirty under any circumstances.

And yet they were changing in a stable. Go figure.

Lainey reached for the zip at Imogen's back and tugged. It stuck at the halfway point for a moment, then slid up. It was a snug fit, but it would do.

"How do I look?" she asked.

Imogen's dress was all black lace and vampy satin—a far cry from her usually sedate approach to fashion. Her jewelled mask hid most of her face, and with a plummy stain coating her usually bare lips, Imogen was transformed.

"Incredible."

"And you…" Imogen squealed. "That hair makes you look like a totally new person."

Lainey had spent years trying to get her naturally dark blond hair to the perfect shade of Gwen Stefani platinum. But earlier that week she'd thrown years of careful bleaching and maintenance down the drain to turn herself into a fiery redhead.

The shade was a vibrant ruby colour that made her fair skin seem even more porcelain. It also warmed up her hazel eyes and gave her total *Little Mermaid* vibes. So much that she was starting to wonder why she'd never been a redhead before.

Imogen reached up to adjust the glittering fabric on Lainey's dress. "You're going to cause trouble for every man in that ballroom."

The skimpy straps and plunging neckline left no room for a bra. And there was a slit up the side of the twinkling silver skirt, which made her feel all kinds of exposed. But that was exactly why she'd picked it. If she was going to do something stupid and reckless, then she was damn well going to look hot while she did it.

"One wrong move and I'm going to flash my boobs," she said with a rueful grin. "Chances are Damian will totally ignore me and I'll end up scandalising Melbourne's society crowd."

"At least you're here for a positive reason," Imogen said. She sounded stressed, though it was hard to tell with the mask covering her face.

"Everything will work out okay. You've thought

this plan through. You're looking after your sister," Lainey said. "But you're not doing anything wrong."

Imogen nodded. "Exactly. I just want to get evidence that he's cheating."

"Wouldn't you'd rather find out he's *not* cheating?" Lainey raised a brow.

Imogen pressed her lips into a flat line. "Don't judge my plans and I won't judge yours, okay?"

"Fair enough." Lainey held her hands up. "I solemnly swear not to mention it again."

"Good." Imogen nodded and scooped up the uniforms they'd worn to sneak into the venue with the owner of the catering company. "We can leave these here and Marie will pick them up later."

Lainey nodded. "What's she getting out of this, by the way?"

"I'm putting her on the preferred suppliers list at work," Imogen said. "We use caterers all the time, so it would be a big chunk of business for her. We're supposed to put all new suppliers through a panel vetting process, but I just told my boss we should use her and he said okay."

"Privilege of being the CEO's right-hand lady?"

"Exactly, and I know she's amazing at her job so I don't feel *too* bad about doing it. You know I don't normally bend the rules, but I figure she's going out on a limb for me…" Guilt flickered across Imogen's expression, but she quickly refocused. "Anyway, let's get this show on the road."

"Knock 'em dead." Lainey gave Imogen's hands a

squeeze and then hung back while her friend headed along the building toward the side entrance.

Imogen paused at the corner, where a path curved through the garden, and peeked around. She held up her hem, a handful of black lace and satin exposing some strappy silver sandals with a sensible midheight heel. Lainey smiled. So there *was* a hint of the real Imogen under her costume.

A second later, Imogen flashed Lainey a thumbs-up. And then she was gone. The plan was for Lainey to count to thirty and then make her way down the same path.

Digging into her clutch, she pulled out a round compact mirror. Unlike the sleek dress, fancy shoes and glamorous mask, the compact was rough around the edges. Well loved. The gold clasp was tarnished and the embroidered rose on the lid had seen better days. But tonight it was her talisman. The compact had belonged to Lainey's grandmother, a woman who'd done fearless things in the name of love. Like giving up marriage to a wealthy aristocrat and forgoing a life of privilege, causing her family to cut her off and cast her out. She'd given it all up for him— her comfort, her security, her family.

She would understand why Lainey was doing something outrageous to have one night with the guy of her dreams.

"One cat dog, two cat dog, three cat dog," Lainey murmured, forcing herself not to speed through her count using the technique her mother had taught her when she was little. "Four cat dog, five cat dog…"

Around twenty cat dogs, she couldn't take it anymore. Touching her fingertips to the black lace mask, she stifled a nervous giggle. Glimmering beads brushed her cheeks every time she moved her head. Combined with the scandalous dress, it made her feel fiercely powerful. Sexy in a way she hadn't ever experienced.

Lainey's high heels made clicking sounds against the stone path. As she turned the corner, a courtyard opened in front of her. The area was large, surrounded by standard white roses and gardenia trees. The scent was intoxicating. Two large glass doors opened to the ballroom, and music spilled out into the air. Lainey's stomach fluttered.

A waiter holding a tray of wineglasses passed by, and she flagged him down. She'd seen him earlier when they'd entered with the catering assistants. But his eyes swept over her without a hint of recognition. *Phew.*

Lainey headed toward the open doors. She wanted to get the lay of the land—see how many people were inside and figure out whether it would be hard to find Damian. The Carmina Ball was in full swing.

Sucking in a breath so big it caused the boning in her dress to dig into her ribs, Lainey stepped into the ballroom. It was like something out of a movie—mysterious masked men in tuxedos, women in incredible gowns, the glittering chandeliers that looked as though they belonged in the castle from *Beauty and the Beast*. It was all her fairy-tale romance-movie dreams come to life.

Was it even real?

She brought her wineglass to her lips, revelling in the flutter of her heart against her rib cage. Yes, it was real. And tonight, she was going to bring her longest-held fantasy to life.

CHAPTER THREE

DAMIAN DIDN'T MIND wearing a suit. Hell, he didn't even mind wearing a tux. But being forced to look like a cross between the Phantom of the Opera and an *Eyes Wide Shut* reject was pushing the limits.

The ballroom of Patterson House stretched out before him, resplendent with gold detailing. The building had been erected in the late 1800s, but the ballroom had been remodelled in the '30s. It was a fitting location for such an event—heaving with history and old money, blue blood to the very core. The women were dressed in spectacular ballgowns and the men in tuxedos. *Everyone* wore a mask. Some were simple scraps of lace or filigree, leaving most of the face bare and recognisable. Others were more ornate, heavily beaded and elaborately designed, a feature of a person's outfit rather than an afterthought.

He tugged at his own black leather mask. It had been designed to resemble a crow, and included sculpted satin feathers. Apparently, it made him look mysterious. That's what he got for letting Aaron's wife pick out a mask for him. But he'd made sure to ask her for one that only covered half his face. He didn't see the point of attending without letting people know he was here, especially since an invite to the Carmina Ball was supposed to be life changing—acceptance from the people who "mattered." A chance to get in with Melbourne's power players.

But the invite had come with strings attached… to the tune of five thousand dollars for entry and expected participation in the night's charitable events. Not that Damian had an issue donating to charity, of course. But he'd told his folks a little white lie about coming tonight so they didn't worry he was frittering away his recently acquired wealth.

"Don't you look handsome," Jessie, Aaron's wife, said as she placed a hand on his arm. "I knew you'd be a good addition to this circle."

"Why, because you wanted some eye candy?" Damian smirked when she slapped her palm lightly against his bicep.

"Watch it," Aaron said, sliding an arm around her waist. "You don't need to worry about me getting jealous, but Jessie plots revenge in the way only a woman can. Hell hath no fury like a grammar girl scorned."

Unlike Damian, both Aaron and Jessie had grown up as part of the elite, with expensive private school educations and safety nets padded with zeros. But regardless of their privilege, both were incredibly hardworking people. He'd met Aaron when they were in their early twenties as graduates at a big four consulting firm, doing grunt work and jumping every time a partner made eye contact. They'd learned the ropes together, climbing the corporate ladder in tandem until Damian left to work at Ben's firm, and he and Aaron had maintained a valuable friendship ever since.

And it was because of Aaron and Jessie that he was here tonight, so he really *should* try to have fun.

"No denial, huh?" Damian said, nudging her with his elbow.

Jessie laughed. "They wouldn't have put you on TV if you didn't look the part."

"Don't encourage him," Aaron muttered. "I had to find an extra ticket so his ego could attend tonight, too."

Damian chuckled and scanned the room. "So, give me the lowdown. Who's who around here?"

"That's Arthur Wentworth and his sons, Parker and Ian," Jessie said. "They own the Wentworth Group. Department stores, luxury vehicles, couture fashion—you name it."

"They're one of my clients," Aaron added. "Don't even think about poaching them."

Damian smiled. Aaron had worked his way up to partner at that firm where they'd started their careers. Some days Damian wondered what might've been if he'd stayed there, too, instead of following Ben. Would he still have his positive attitude...or his wife?

"I won't dip my hand in the cookie jar, I promise," he drawled.

"Who else would be of interest?" Jessie clucked her tongue. "The Allbrook family is here—they own a huge architecture firm that does a lot of high-end

residential towers in the city. We've got judges, poli-
ticians, CEOs, barristers, even a few celebrities. I
heard a rumour that Cate Blanchett might be coming."

"Excellent. I'll ask for her autograph," Damian
said with a straight face.

Jessie looked horrified for a moment before she
realised he was joking. "Damian, please."

"Your South Yarra is showing," he said. "You
might want to cover that up."

"Not here." Aaron chuckled. "It's practically a re-
quirement for entry."

Jessie rolled her eyes and pushed on, pointing out
people across the room. "Oh, and my friend Amelia
told me the restaurateur Jerry McPartlin is going to
be here. I ate at his new place, Gilt, last week. It was
absolutely divine."

Damian's ears pricked up, ignoring Aaron, who
was giving him a stern look. "Really?"

Suddenly, the evening had gotten a whole lot more
interesting. This would be the perfect opportunity for
him to chat with the uptight family man in a social
setting and try to figure out exactly what he needed
to do to secure the guy's business.

Did he need a girlfriend? A fiancée? Promise to
give up his firstborn? Whatever it was, Damian was
ready to sign on the dotted line. Snagging McPartlin
& Co. would be the best possible thing he could do,
because another big-name client was extra security.
Relying only on one or two big fish meant your business balanced on a knife's edge, and keeping the client

happy often overtook the uncomfortable but necessary process of crafting the right solution for them.

The fact was, any big client would help him. But he *wanted* this one.

Signing McPartlin & Co. would give him the closure he needed to finally shut the door on his past. Or rather, slam it in the faces of those who'd broken his heart.

A while later, Damian stood at the edge of the crowd, watching. He felt like a kid at the zoo, his face pressed against the glass of the reptile enclosure. Everything happening in front of him was foreign. Alien. This wasn't his world...yet.

Sure, he was rich by most people's standards. He lived in a luxury hotel that cost more per week than what he'd spent on his first car. But that would be nothing to these people.

And he knew that an evening like this could make or break him. Get the right connections and his business would soar. Piss off the wrong person and... well, he could easily be back to doing grunt work for some asshole.

Damian clenched his fists and let the fantasy of punching his ex-boss in the face roll through him like a wave. The betrayal was no less raw today than it had been four years ago when he'd come back to the office late one night to pick up his laptop and found his wife spread-eagled on Ben's desk.

The Carmina Ball was the key to it all. To revenge. To *closure*.

If only he could get close to Jerry McPartlin.

The man stood a few metres away, surrounded by a group of women who wore dresses so large they created a barrier around him. And it looked like he was loving the attention, too. Damian could wait. Patience and determination were two of his greatest strengths, and he would find the perfect moment to strike. Before the night was out, he *would* have a plan.

"I wasn't expecting to find such good company playing wallflower," a silky voice said.

A woman sidled up to him, her shimmering mask of white lace studded with gems that winked at him. Black hair flowed over one shoulder in stark contrast to a floor-length white ballgown. Her full lips were painted red and they curved into an inviting smile.

"That depends. What kind of company are you looking for?" He stuck out his hand. "I'm Damian."

"Hannah," the woman replied. "You have a familiar face."

Ugh. He could almost guarantee what was coming next, the one sentence that made him cringe every bloody time.

You're that guy from Australia's Most Eligible.

But instead she cocked her head, the gems on her mask shimmering, and said nothing.

He was about to respond when a blur of red stole the words from his mouth. Moisture soaked through Damian's dress shirt and the sound of glass shattering pierced the subtle din of the ballroom. He'd been hit.

"Oh my God." A woman with blazing-red hair reached out to touch his chest, her fingertips sending fire through his veins. "I am so sorry."

Damian looked down. Wine streaked his chest, a slash of angry red against the crisp white cotton. The broken glass glittered in a pool of liquid on the floor, its stem rolling across the parquet.

"You got me good." He brushed his hands over his chest in a futile attempt to clean himself up.

"Excuse me." The redhead waved to get the attention of a waiter, but there was already a small army descending to clean up the mess.

Her silver gown was bunched in one hand, revealing a finely boned ankle encased in a strappy, high-heeled shoe. She tried to take a step but couldn't shift her full weight onto her foot.

"You might have some glass in your shoe," he said, reaching out to her. "Come on. Let's get you cleaned up."

She accepted his hand. Her mask was so detailed it was impossible to see much of her face—it covered her entirely from above her brows to above her lips. "I'm so sorry, my hem got caught…"

Damian narrowed his eyes at the sound of her voice. It was familiar, but he couldn't place it. Maybe she was a business acquaintance? Or someone he'd met during filming? She seemed the glamorous type who might be part of the entertainment industry. But without seeing her face, it would be impossible to tell, and there couldn't be too many people he knew who could afford the Carmina Ball's ticket price.

Plus, he was *sure* he would have remembered a woman with hair the colour of rubies. A woman whose touch stirred something impossibly primal and strange inside him.

He looped her arm around his neck and supported her slight weight. But a few hobbling steps later, when it was clear she was frightened to put pressure on her foot, he lifted her into his arms and strode through the ballroom with what felt like the whole city watching.

CHAPTER FOUR

BROKEN GLASS AND bloodshed weren't supposed to be part of the deal. Not to mention the fact that she'd come precariously close to getting red wine on her borrowed finery. But it was the stupid dress that caused the problem in the first place. Who was tall enough for these damn dresses? Amazonians?

The fabric had gotten caught under her heel and she'd stumbled, the wine splashing across Damian as the glass escaped her grip. She was only supposed to slosh a little over the edge, just enough to interrupt him and the glamorous woman in the white dress who was about to go in for the kill.

But oh no. That would have been too easy, and Lainey never could seem to take the easy route.

So elegant, Kline. Like a drunk baby llama on roller skates.

But being weightless in Damian's arms was more than she could have hoped for, at least within the first five minutes. Now all she had to do was cross her fingers that she hadn't embedded glass in her foot.

"You okay?" he asked as they exited the ballroom and headed to the powder rooms.

The mask covered only half of his face, one eye and cheek, Phantom of the Opera–style. That was how she'd spotted him so easily. Tonight he was freshly shaven, his olive skin smooth. By the end of the night he'd have a shadow there, a hint of darkness impressing itself on his clean-cut image. Like a reminder that he was more than he appeared.

"I'm not about to pass out from blood loss, if that's what you mean," she replied in the voice she'd been practising all week. She spoke slower and breathier than normal, trying to disguise the very last thing that could give her away.

"I should hope not." His tone was heavy with amusement. "I doubt they'll take the tux back if it's got blood on it."

A five-thousand-dollar entry price and Damian had rented a tuxedo? For some reason that made her grin like an idiot. No matter how rich he got, there would always be a hint of where he came from lurking beneath. And damn if that didn't make her heart swell.

No hearts, no flowers, no chocolates. Cut that shit out right now. This is a fantasy. Nothing more.

"At least you'd have a story to tell."

"I have a lot of stories to tell. That's not my problem."

"What *is* your problem?" Her heartbeat kicked up a notch when his eyes shifted down to hers. With the black surrounds of the mask, the sharp blue of his irises was even more stark and breathtaking. "Maybe I can help."

The corner of his lip quirked. "You'll do the opposite of that, I'm afraid."

"Try me. You never know when a stranger might be exactly what you need."

A little seed of guilt unfurled in her stomach. She was no stranger and everything about this encounter was for her own selfish gain—to appease the fantasy that'd plagued her for years.

You're not forcing him to do anything. If this goes somewhere, it'll be because he accepts your offer, not because you held a gun to his head.

They reached the private powder rooms. There were no cubicles for the guests of Patterson House, that was for damn sure. Each powder room was spacious, with a single private sink and toilet. Lainey thanked her lucky stars for the diva-like needs of the rich, because it would afford them some privacy.

Holding her, Damian nudged the door open with his foot and let it swing shut behind him. The click of the automatic latch was like a single firework in the quiet room, the sound echoing off the tiles and rattling around in her brain. He set her on the marble countertop. Lainey glanced around. The room was like no other bathroom she'd ever seen—the taps were gold and ornate, and fresh flowers sat in a vase that was most likely crystal. They even had a fancy hand soap dispenser that resembled a Fabergé egg.

"Let's have a look at the damage." He crouched in front of her, pushing her dress up so he could get to her foot. His fingers made quick work of the strap on her sandal, and with one hand bracing her ankle, he slipped the shoe off.

The action was so soft and caring that Lainey's heart caught in her throat. The warmth of his fingers was like an aphrodisiac, potent. Intoxicating. Her blood hummed at the contrast of it all—the firmness of his grip mixed with the careful, tender touch.

"I think you can keep the foot," he said, his tone serious. But the twinkle in his eye gave him away.

It appeared Damian *did* still have a sense of humour, much to her delight.

"You think?" Lainey peered down and wriggled her toes. The light glinted off the shimmery black nail polish she'd chosen because it reminded her of the stars against a night sky. "The word *think* isn't something I want to hear when we're discussing amputation."

He chuckled and lifted her foot higher to inspect the sole. "I'm going to rub my thumb across the ball of your foot. If you feel any pain, then there could be glass under the skin."

She nodded, her breath stuttering like a car engine failing to turn over. Lainey wasn't sure she'd be able to detect pain—or anything else—as Damian inspected her. For an encounter that shouldn't have been in the least bit sexual, every nerve ending in her body was singing as though it was Christmas Day and New Year's Eve and every other damn holiday all at once.

"Do you feel anything?" He looked up.

Seeing a big man like him on his knees, looking

up at her through that sexier-than-sin mask, touching her as though she were the most precious thing in all the world…

"I think I'd be a statue not to feel something," she said, her voice low and soft. "But I'm not in pain."

He held on to her foot for a moment, his eyes fixed on her. Her calf was cradled in his palm, the heat from his skin working its way through her, turning her veins to threads of fire. Thank God she had a mask on so he couldn't see her face heating up. They stayed there—locked in that moment, frozen by intimacy—until he cleared his throat and slipped the shoe back onto her foot.

"So I'll be alright, Doc?"

"Better than alright." He stood. The tuxedo fit him perfectly, hugging his shoulders and tapering down to his waist in a line so mouthwateringly divine, it stole Lainey's breath. The only thing ruining the effect was the red wine stain. "I'm glad we checked—the last thing you want is a glass splinter."

"Exactly. Cinderella had glass on her feet, and look how that turned out."

He raised a brow. "She got the prince, didn't she?"

"The prince had to rely on the fit of a shoe." Lainey shook her head. "What she got was a dude with a bad memory and a foot fetish."

Damian chuckled. "Not into fairy tales, then?"

"Oh, I am." She swung her feet, relishing the swish of the beaded material around her ankles. "But Cinderella isn't my favourite. What woman wants a man who can't remember her face?"

"Good point." He pulled a hand towel out of a small basket beside the sink and ran it under water. "They're all kind of messed up when you think about it. Sleeping Beauty, especially."

"I prefer my romances a little more grounded in reality." Lainey swallowed as Damian dabbed at the stain on his shirt, turning the fabric damp so that it clung to his chest muscles.

If bodies were supposed to be temples, his was the Parthenon.

Maybe if you'd been able to recall that kind of crap during exams instead of checking out a hot guy, you would have done better at school.

"Do you mean the kind of movies where the woman splashes the man with red wine and seduces him in a bathroom?" He caught her gaze in the mirror.

"I haven't seduced you yet."

"Yet." His smile turned from amused to wolfish, his lips revealing a perfect set of white teeth. "So there's still hope."

"You don't even know my name."

No, he didn't know her name. And he was supposed to be focused on seducing his client, not a mysterious redhead. But having her alone, feeling her energy sparking all around him put him in his element. Not like out there, where he was an anomaly.

If she's here, then she's one of them. A rich princess type who'll be more trouble than she's worth.

Just like his ex.

But something gave him pause. There was an inkling, more the potential for a feeling than a feeling itself, that said he was wrong. When she'd dropped her glass, the first thing out of her mouth had been an apology—not an excuse or accusation. When he'd offered her help, she'd graciously accepted. And now she was teasing him. Playing with him.

The redhead was like him, an outsider looking in. He knew it.

"Maybe I can guess your name," he said, giving up on the stained shirt and throwing the face towel into the basket below the sink. "Wasn't that in a fairy tale?"

"Rumpelstiltskin. It's not a very romantic one." Her legs swung back and forth over the edge of the marble countertop. Though they didn't know each other, she seemed completely at ease. "But you can try. I'll give you three guesses, and if you lose…" She tapped a finger against her chin. "You have to share a drink with me on the balcony upstairs."

He braced his hands against the countertop, leaning toward her. She smelled like vanilla and peaches. The black beads on her mask glittered, reflecting his hungry expression in miniature, over and over.

"How many names are there in the world? I'd be a fool to take such a bet." He grinned. "Do I get any clues?"

"You don't look like a man who needs a clue."

"Some might argue that," he said drily. Damian himself thought a clue would be good right about now—one that would give him the hint to leave this woman alone and head back out to the ballroom so he could corner Jerry McPartlin.

She turned to look in the mirror for a moment. "My name has nothing to do with my hair colour."

"So not Ruby or Scarlett or Rose?"

"Nope." She tucked a strand of fiery-red hair behind her ear.

"That doesn't really narrow it down. Can I get a letter?"

"This isn't *Wheel of Fortune*."

His lip quirked. "How about a year of birth?"

"Tsk, tsk." She waggled a finger at him. "That's the one thing you should never ask a lady."

He thought for a moment, cycling through some options that would be appropriate for someone in her age group—which was tough to narrow down without being able to see most of her face. But from the smooth, unblemished skin and the way she sat, comfortable and swinging her feet…he'd put her at her midtwenties. Maybe less, although he didn't want to think about her being over a decade younger than him.

"You're holding all the cards."

She grinned. "Which is exactly how I like it."

"You're not a negotiator, are you?"

"No. I'm a romantic and a dreamer."

"Ah, so you're unemployed?"

She threw her head back and laughed, the sound striking him right in the chest. But it cut off before he could grasp hold of something that flickered out of reach. A memory.

"Do we know each other?" he asked, looking closer.

"No." The answer was immediate, her reaction drawing a line between them that made him curious as hell.

"Will you take your mask off before I guess?" He cocked his head. "Help me even the playing field a little?"

"Tonight is all about the mystery, don't you think? Strangers without faces."

Ah, so she was looking for something anonymous. He wasn't sure why that unsettled him—hell, *he'd* looked for exactly that on countless occasions. No names, no phone numbers. No repeats.

And certainly no fucking regrets.

Maybe it was because Jerry McPartlin had gotten Damian's head all messed up, but he accepted her terms. "Okay, three guesses it is."

She drew her bottom lip between her teeth, as though stifling a grin. The mysterious redhead knew she was going to win, little minx. She held up three fingers. "Go on."

"Is it…Samantha?"

One finger curled down toward her palm. "Strike one."

"How about…Natalie?"

She shook her head. "Strike two."

"Lucky last guess." He blew out a breath, enjoying the way she shifted on the countertop, a faint flush colouring her chest. "Amanda?"

She made a buzzer noise and dropped her hand down. "You owe me a drink now."

He wanted something else. No doubt she would taste better than the top-shelf stuff they were serving in the ballroom. A drink seemed far too tame for her lush, full lips and creamy skin. For that bold, flaming hair and the dress that was cut to a deep V at her chest. For the slit that flashed a shapely leg and hinted at sex and sinfulness.

He stood in front of her, his hands falling to the countertop on either side of her thighs, hemming her in. He watched her pupils flare—no fear, just desire. Her chest rose and fell with quickened breath, and her lips eased open a fraction. Taunting him. Inviting him in.

Lust battled with logic—telling him to stay and kiss her. To leave and go after Jerry McPartlin.

A series of thumps rattled the door to the bathroom, frantic and quick. "Excuse me? Is anyone in there?"

Damian stepped back and helped the redhead down from the countertop. "Looks like that's our cue to go. Can you walk okay now?"

She nodded. "Yeah."

He opened the door, allowing the redhead to exit before him. A man in an elaborate gold mask bounced up and down on the spot, clutching his stomach. He pushed past Damian and the redhead with an angry huff. "You know these bathrooms aren't for fooling around. Some people have to *use* them."

Giggling, the redhead grabbed his hand and pulled him down the corridor, away from the ballroom, to a grand curving staircase. "Come on, this way."

"I don't think there's anything up there, Ariel."

"So that's my name now?" The hazel of her irises shifted in the light, making the small amber flecks look like gold dust. "Ariel?"

"Seems fitting. Long red hair, mysteriously showing up out of nowhere." His eyes dropped down. "Great legs."

She laughed and tugged him farther along. The back of the corridor was deserted, but the sound of clanging grew louder. Just before they hit the staircase, a waiter exited from a swinging door, his uniform crisply pressed. The redhead marched right into the kitchen, as bold and brazen as anything, and plucked two champagne flutes from a silver tray that was waiting to go out.

"What are you doing?" he asked as she breezed back into the hallway as though it were totally normal for ball gown–clad guests to steal drinks.

"There's no service upstairs." She handed him a flute. "Come on, you promised me a drink on the balcony."

Damian looked toward the entrance to the ballroom, where a group of men in tuxedos were gathered. Their rich, booming laughter floated down the hall, the sound of stuffy voices discussing boring things ringing in the air.

Last chance. Go back in there and work on your plan. Or be the man McPartlin thinks you are.

The redhead leaned in close, the beaded strands on her mask brushing his cheek. Warm breath whispered over his skin as the scent of her perfume grabbed hold of his heart. "You know you want to and *I* know you want to."

He turned, his face so close to hers he could have captured her mouth. "Fine," he said. "One drink."

CHAPTER FIVE

LAINEY'S HEART HAMMERED like a toddler beating tin pots together, the feeling vibrating through her body right down to her thankfully uninjured toes. That moment in the bathroom, where Damian had asked if they knew one another, she'd thought it was all over.

James Bond she was not.

But her response must have satisfied him, because his suspicion had drained away.

Holding her hem tightly in one hand, she lifted the fabric as they ascended to the next floor of Patterson House. According to the little sign at the bottom of the stairs that politely directed guests back to the ballroom, the balcony was supposed to be off-limits. But Lainey figured if they really wanted people to stay downstairs, they would have roped it off.

In any case, she needed to get Damian in private again. He'd been about to kiss her before that bumbling idiot and his digestive issues had interrupted them. She was sure of it. And that kiss was dancing in her head. She wanted it. Bad.

As they stepped out onto the balcony, warm air

swept over Lainey's skin, reminding her how much she had on display. A shiver rippled through her.

"It's a beautiful house," Damian said.

"It is."

The balcony was as ornate as the rest of the building. White fretwork closed the balcony in while letting light filter through. The sun had started to set, and shades of orange and pink streaked the sky, making the greenery of the Patterson House gardens seem all the more vibrant. Lainey felt like a star waiting for nightfall.

"Cheers." Damian held his glass up, and she clinked her own against it. "Here's to masked strangers and wayward wineglasses."

"And fairy tales and guessing games." She sipped her drink.

"I notice you haven't asked for *my* name," he said.

Shit. She'd been too busy worrying about protecting her own identity that she'd momentarily forgotten that she wasn't supposed to know him.

"You're awfully hung up on names," she replied, walking to the edge of the balcony and peering down at the garden below.

"And you're awfully evasive." He smiled, his head tilted slightly. She recognised that look; he was trying to figure her out.

"Let's just say that being able to wear a mask was the reason I decided to come here tonight."

The scent of gardenias floated past on a breeze. The balcony overlooked the garden rather than the courtyard, and she could see two people stealing away.

Was it Imogen? Lainey tried to get a better look, but the haze of dusk made it hard to tell.

"Are you hiding from someone?" he asked. "Or pretending to be someone else?"

"A little from column A and a little from column B." She took another sip of her champagne. "And that's the truth. I'm not trying to be evasive."

"You can still be things even if you're not trying." His lip quirked. "Tell me, Ariel. If you're not yourself tonight, who are you?"

He was close. So close she could smell the cologne on his skin and the bare hint of his soap underneath. He'd used the same sandalwood soap since forever. The clean, woodsy notes were burned into her brain—and never ceased to shock her with a mix of memory and fantasy.

The visuals played like a film reel in her head, flickering images from that day years ago when she'd been studying at Corinna's place. She'd watched him strip down to his board shorts and dive into their pool. She'd imagined what would come next. Following him into the water, pulling him close, running her hand over his naked chest...

"I'm no one."

He reached for her champagne and placed the two flutes on a table. Then he did the same with her clutch. It was like being stripped down, and her empty hands felt naked without something to do. "You are most certainly *someone*."

"Maybe I'm a figment of your imagination."

"I hope not." His voice lowered, the sound rough yet silky. Like satin dragging over gravel.

Her breath hitched as his fingertips came to her waist, confident and firm. With the dress sucking her in, his hands looked enormous against her. He could overpower her, control her. She wanted him to.

The voice in her head shouted at her to press against him, but she wanted to draw this moment out. Stretch it like toffee and give her brain time to soak in every minute detail. This moment would have to sustain her for the rest of her life and become the thing she could cling to late at night. Her fantasy come to life. She couldn't—*wouldn't*—rush it.

"Why?" Her hands came to his chest.

Beneath the thick cotton of his dress shirt, he felt like sculpted stone. Hard and unyielding. Powerful. She had to remind herself to breathe, not to lose herself entirely and let something slip. Like his name.

"Because imagining things is a waste of time. Why spend energy on something that isn't real?" His hand slid around her back, pulling her closer.

"Life doesn't always measure up to a fantasy." Her voice was barely a whisper now, thin and soft and unnatural. The rest of her body struggled to function with all the adrenaline coursing through her veins.

"That's sad, Ariel."

"It's the truth." Not just that, it was the story of her freaking life. The world she'd created in her head—the world that matched the romantic stories she loved so much—was *way* better than reality. If real life truly lived up to her fantasies, then she wouldn't be wearing a mask tonight.

His head lowered to hers, hovering for what felt like her life three times over, before he ended the torture. He crushed her to him, his lips landing on hers and opening in a hot kiss, delving and exploring and tasting. Making her head spin and the world shift beneath her feet.

God help her, she was done for. Ruined for all other men. For all other kisses.

His lips were soft and full, the taste of champagne and the scent of something earthy and male lingering in her senses. Heaven. Her hand found the back of his head and her fingers thrust into his hair, pulling him closer, hoping it might stop her from levitating in his arms. From floating up into the night air.

When his hand slipped up her thigh, parting the slit in her dress, her body sang out: yes, yes, *yes*.

She ached everywhere. In her head, in her heart, between her legs. For him. Because of him.

His palm was hot against her skin, his thumb moving in slow circles against her inner thigh. Inching higher, then retreating. Moving forward and back in a maddening, teasing dance that left her breathless with need. She tightened her grip while her tongue ran along his lower lip. She nipped at him, dragging a groan from deep in his throat. The sound rubbed her nerve endings raw, heightening her sensitivity.

He kissed her as if all of his pent-up lust and attraction and protective urges spilled forth at once. As if he'd fantasised about this for the past decade just as she had. This was everything she'd wanted, and holy *hell* did it live up to expectation.

"My God," she groaned into his mouth, thrusting her body forward so their chests pressed together.

He backed her up against the railing, keeping one arm around her waist and pushing his other hand up higher so he could slide it around to cup her ass. Warm air caressed her everywhere, the tiny scrap of lace masquerading as underwear covering only the necessities. He moaned into her mouth as he grabbed bare flesh.

"You feel so damn good," he gritted out as his teeth scraped along her neck. "And you taste like heaven."

"Touch me," she whispered into his ear. "Please."

He traced the lines of her body, the curves of her hips, and felt for the heat between her legs. Pinpoints of light danced behind her shuttered lids as he finally brushed his fingers over her sex. The thin silk and lace of her underwear hid nothing. He crushed his lips against hers, kissing her rough and hard and dirty. With teeth and tongue. Ferocious. Demanding. Every cell in her body fired as if fighting for life. Fighting for survival. Fighting to hang on for that one moment of pleasure.

"Please," she whimpered. "I need more."

"The next step is you coming against my hand, princess." The growl in his voice rippled over her skin. "Because once I start, I won't stop until you're shaking with my fingers inside you."

"Yes," she gasped as he toyed with the edge of her

underwear, the back of his knuckle rubbing against her sex.

"Be sure." His teeth were at her neck, scraping the line from her jaw to her collarbone.

"I am." Her eyes fluttered shut. "I couldn't be surer. I am *so* sure right now."

He chuckled against her neck. "I like a woman who knows what she wants."

"And I like a man who's good with his hands." She arched her back as he pushed her underwear to the side, biting down on her lower lip to keep from crying out.

The last thing she wanted was to attract the attention of the people milling below. But it was hard not to let the groans fall from her mouth as he stroked her. Played with her. His fingers pressed into her, dragging the moisture from inside her sex and rubbing it over her clit. Her whole body throbbed.

"That's it." He dragged one of her legs over his hip to open her further. "Let me feel how wet you are."

His hand moved against her sex, his thumb strumming the swollen bud of her clit like he knew exactly how to make her fly. The edge of release rushed toward her, tremors starting in her thighs and spreading out, until it felt like she was going to fall. But his other hand held her steady, cradled her with a gentleness that belied the demanding fingers between her legs.

"It's too soon," she gasped, trying to hold on— to draw it out—but he knew her body too well. *Way* too well.

"It's perfect, princess." He pressed his lips to her temple. "Don't fight it."

She couldn't, even if she'd wanted to. Release rose up from her depths and blanked everything out—sound, sight, smell. It was all lost. Nothing but the electric feel of the orgasm rocketing through her.

Her hands clasped his head, her nails biting into his scalp as she tried so very hard to muffle her cries against his neck. His voice broke through as the intensity ebbed, soft and low. A whisper.

Princess.

She melted in his arms, liquid in the wake of her pleasure. But he had her. She wouldn't fall.

"That was so fucking beautiful," he whispered, grabbing her hand and bringing it down to his cock. He was like marble, hard and rigid beneath her trembling fingers. "You got me all worked up."

She righted herself, smoothing her dress down with one hand and keeping her other on him as his body pinned her to the balcony railing. "I did?"

"Those quiet little cries as you came are going to haunt me for the rest of my life."

She swallowed. This man…he was everything she'd known he'd be. Her body and soul were alive, filled with a satisfaction so vibrant, she wondered why she'd never realised that she was only half-awake before.

But when she opened her mouth to respond, the sound of footsteps froze her.

"Ahem." Three men stood at the edge of the balcony, all in tuxedos and without masks. "Looks like we're interrupting something," the one in the middle said.

Lainey wanted to shout that they were and tell them to get lost. Her perfect moment with Damian had been interrupted, and for what? So these beefcakes could judge them? She had to fight the urge to slap the smarmy smirk off the middle guy's face.

"Looks like you are," Damian said.

"Can I see your ticket?" one of the goons asked.

Lainey's heart leapt into her chest. She hadn't counted on being asked for her ticket once she was *inside* the venue. Crap. How was she going to explain that issue away?

"We've had a report of someone sneaking into the event," goon number two added. "We take the privacy of our guests very seriously."

Damian slipped his hand into the inside pocket of his jacket and handed his invite over. *Mr. Damian Edward McKnight* was written in scrolled font across thick cream paper. Lainey would bet money they'd spent more on having the invites printed than she forked out for rent each year.

"Damian McKnight," he confirmed. "My apologies to have to interrupt you, Mr. McKnight. I'm sure you understand that we have to take these matters seriously."

Damian nodded. "Of course."

Just as the goons turned to Lainey, someone came up behind them. This man was in a mask, so obviously he wasn't one of the security staff.

"I thought I heard a familiar name," he said. "I was

coming up here to get away from the crowd, and it looks like you two had the same idea."

"Mr. McPartlin." Damian's tone was flat.

As in Jerry McPartlin. *The* Jerry McPartlin. Lainey knew his name because her parents were huge fans of his first restaurant, Ora. They couldn't afford to eat there regularly, but once a year on their wedding anniversary, they splurged.

"Are you going to introduce me to your lovely guest?" Jerry motioned to Lainey.

Fuck. Of *course* it had to be Jerry McPartlin who stumbled across him with a gorgeous, nameless girl in his arms in an area of the building they weren't supposed to be in. He and the redhead had broken apart the second the security team had walked in, but why else would two people be hiding up here on a private balcony? Any hope he had of changing the man's opinion had vanished into thin air. Unless...

An idea sprang to his mind. Hadn't he been saying to Aaron that he needed to look like a family man? Like a guy who'd finally settled down?

This was either going to work brilliantly, or everything he wanted—needed—was going to come crashing down around him. Saying nothing would mean certain failure, and his motto had always been Go Big or Go Home.

"I'd like to introduce you to my fiancée, Ariel." He squeezed the redhead's hands in what he hoped was a silent plea for her to go along with his plan.

"Your fiancée?" Jerry cocked his head. "You never mentioned that you were getting married."

Damian glanced at the woman beside him, who'd stayed mercifully quiet. "Didn't think it was a necessary part of doing business."

"It's a pleasure." Jerry stuck out his hand, and the redhead hesitated a moment before accepting the gesture.

"Likewise. I'm a huge fan your restaurants, Mr. McPartlin."

"Please, call me Jerry." He kissed the back of her hand before looking back at Damian. "Charming and glamorous. Looks like you're a lucky man."

"Not lucky enough to secure your business, on account of my image." He couldn't resist the little barb, especially since it appeared as though his story had been bought. "You can't blame a man for wanting to steal a moment away with his soon-to-be wife, can you?"

"Perhaps I was too quick to judge." His gaze lingered on the redhead's hand, which wasn't wearing a ring. "Didn't you propose with a diamond?"

Shit. His mind whirred again.

"We're having something custom-made," she said, her voice silky smooth as though she hadn't been panting and breathless a few moments ago. "Damian knows how much I like things to be perfect."

She knew his name? He turned to the woman and her face tilted up to him, her lips full and pink. They curved into a smile. Of course, the security staff had said it aloud when they'd checked his invite. At least

that bit of detail could lend extra authenticity to their
story.

"That's my Ariel." He slipped an arm around her
shoulders and drew her close. He sensed McPartlin's
eye lingering on her. "She knows exactly what she
wants."

"Well, I'm glad we cleared that up." McPartlin
nodded.

"We still need to check your invite, miss," one of
the security guys said.

The redhead stiffened beside him. Her hand tightened around his, squeezing in a way that told Damian
she was *exactly* who they were looking for. No wonder she wasn't keen to give up her name.

"I'm afraid Ariel's invite met with an unfortunate
end," he said. "In the bathroom."

The guards looked at one another, unsure how to
handle that information.

"It's my fault," the redhead said, her voice perfectly pleasing and yet slightly breathy. "I was at the
sink and my clutch got caught and spilled open."

"It's not your fault, darling." He rubbed her back in
slow circles, the role of doting fiancé taking him over
fully. A wicked smile curved on his lips. "I shouldn't
have been so rough."

A small gasp sounded on her lips, but it was cut
off by one of the guards clearing his throat. "Well,
then. We should get moving."

"It was great to see you again." Damian nodded to
McPartlin as he turned to leave, as well.

"Yes." The older man looked them both over once

more, as if trying to figure something out. "Enjoy the evening."

Damian and the redhead stood close together on the balcony without saying a word until the men had descended to the ground level. Her relief was palpable in the evening air, and she sagged against him.

"So you're a gate-crasher, huh?" Damian glanced down into her wide hazel eyes. "That's a bold move. This is a very important event."

"It certainly is," she replied smoothly. "Oh, dear future husband of mine."

He chuckled. Neither one of them was in a position to judge—they were both liars. Or both saviours, depending on how you looked at it.

"I guess this means I'm stuck with you for the rest of the evening, then?" she said, resting her head against his arm.

"Looks that way."

He could think of worse ways to spend an evening—and at least having company would keep him from going crazy with all the snobbery in the ballroom. However, he'd put himself into a tight spot with Jerry McPartlin. While letting the man think he had a fiancée could work to his advantage, he'd have to make sure that Jerry McPartlin didn't need to see his "future wife" ever again.

CHAPTER SIX

LAINEY COULDN'T BELIEVE her luck. Damian had practically done all the work for her—the whole thing about her being his fake fiancée meant they *had* to spend the evening together. And since he was the one who'd made that happen, she'd been able to relax and enjoy his company.

Or, more accurately, quietly freak out and enjoy his company.

They'd danced, eaten tiny, fanciful foods; she watched him bid on the silent auctions and talk to people whose names she knew from the papers. There'd been a lot of business talk, too. But he continued to introduce her as his fiancée, Ariel, and so that meant playing the supportive, doting future Mrs. McKnight. Of course, they'd had to explain the ruse to his friends, who'd eyed her with suspicion.

Now they were in the ballroom, and Lainey had her arms looped around his neck while his hand pressed into her lower back. It wasn't dancing, per se. More like swaying in time with the music. But Lainey could have died right that second and been the happiest person on earth. Even in the whole Milky Way. This was the night of her dreams...but hopefully with a dirtier ending.

"You know what this means, don't you?" he asked.

"What?" She tilted her face up to his.

"We need to leave together." He'd bowed his head, his lips brushing her ear as the gravelly words made her knees go weak. "In case people are watching."

"Of course."

Damian held her close, his hand smoothing over her lower back, exposed by her dress. "No protest? I could be anyone."

"So could I." Her fingertips found his jaw, tracing the hard angle softened by smooth skin. "But that's the whole point of a masquerade ball. We get to be anyone we want for a night."

"Why did you come here?"

"I was hoping to get swept off my feet." She grinned. "But a fake proposal will have to do."

"If memory serves me correctly, I literally did sweep you off your feet. I might even have saved your foot."

"That's not what I meant."

His forehead pressed against hers, mask to mask. Beads brushed her skin as she tilted up to him, her lips hovering a hairbreadth from his.

"What did you mean, Ariel? You wanted a man who was going to whisk you away to his castle and turn you into a princess?"

"No." She shook her head. "I wanted a man who

was going to treat me like a queen right now. A fantasy for one night—that's all I want."

Something stormy and electric shifted in his eyes, his lips tightening. But Damian wasn't a man to hide his feelings. His hands shifted lower, cupping her behind and pressing her flush against him. He was harder than an algebra exam.

"One night?" he growled in her ear. "And nothing more?"

"I promise to turn into a pumpkin at twelve on the dot." She dented her lower lip with her teeth, desperate to rub against him—to get the friction her body cried out for—but trying not to draw attention to them any more than they already had. This obviously wasn't the kind of dancing the Carmina Ball was used to. "Then you'll never hear from me again."

"That's really what you want?"

No. She wanted what he'd said—for him to whisk her away and make her his. For that proposal to be real. For the lust in his eyes to be something more. But Lainey was a pragmatist, if nothing else. And she knew there was no point wanting what she couldn't have.

"Yes," she lied. "That's exactly what I want."

His hands dropped suddenly and she stepped back, her body raging at the loss of contact. Her need chanted like a drumbeat in her bloodstream: *more, more, more.* The rushing sound in her ears drowned out the rest of the ballroom, her focus narrowing to him. Only him.

He was like a strange man-god hybrid in his black

tuxedo and mask. The curve of the design high-lighted his perfect nose—aquiline and aristocratic—the black leather making him darkly handsome. His lips formed a smile that sent a tremor through her. It wasn't friendly, wasn't romantic or caring or any of the other smiles she'd seen in the past. It was preda-tory. Delicious.

"Let's go." He held out his hand. "Now."

Lainey glanced around the room—the ball was coming to an end. Guests were already leaving, though the waiters still lingered with drinks on their trays. "Now?"

"Right now. I've done enough business for one night." He grabbed her hand and pulled her to his side, his head dropping down to her ear. "And if we don't finish this soon, I'm liable to drag you behind one of those potted plants in the next few seconds."

"That could be fun," she teased.

"I don't like being quiet, Ariel." Each word tugged on her nerves. He was playing her like a harp. "When I'm inside you, I want to make as much noise as I can so you know how incredible you feel wrapped around my cock."

Her breath stuttered. Holy. Freaking. Shit. Damian wasn't a man god—he was pure sexual divinity. That one sentence had taken her from being excited and warm on the inside to drenching her lacy underwear. He was right, they had to go now. Because that potted plant was starting to look like the perfect place to be.

"Hurry up, then." She strode away from him. "Time's a-wasting."

Chuckling, he followed her to the front of Patterson House. The grand foyer was a sight to behold—an intricate parquet floor gleaming under an enormous chandelier that looked like something straight out of a royal palace. Two security guards stood by the front door, but Lainey couldn't tell if they were the ones who'd caught them on the balcony.

They joined a short queue of people leaving the building, and Lainey tapped her foot impatiently.

"Good evening, sir," a man in a dark suit said as they reached the front of the line. "Can we get you a car or do you have one booked?"

Damian nodded. "A car would be great, thank you."

The man stepped out onto the path that framed the circular driveway in front of the estate and raised a hand. A moment later, a black limousine appeared.

She'd never been in a limo before—never had a reason to. Her life hadn't been littered with special occasions that required fancy dresses and fancy cars and drivers who held the door.

"After you." Damian motioned for her to enter first.

She slid onto the seat as elegantly as she could, the length of her dress in one hand and her clutch in the other. Damian followed her, and the bang of the door filled her with electricity. With excitable, nervous energy. She pulled her grandmother's compact out of her bag and touched up her gloss, because she had no idea what was supposed to happen next.

Her plans had never taken her this far, because, in

the back of her mind, she'd been certain she would fail. Or be discovered. Or that he would have no interest in her, even with the disguise.

But he did.

"They went all out," she said, snapping the compact shut and running her thumb over the embroidery. "Limousines for that many guests must have cost a fortune."

"Well, the ticket holders pay for it, really. Not that you would know that." His lip quirked. "How did you get past security, anyway?"

"I would tell you, but..." She shrugged. "You know how it goes."

"Blood and mayhem and all that."

"Exactly. Don't make me ruin such a pretty dress."

"If that dress is going to be ruined, it won't be by bloodshed. Trust me." He leaned back and stretched his arm along the back of the leather seat. The pose—coupled with the way his gaze burned her up—was so unabashedly male. She'd always envied his confidence in the space he occupied. "Now the mask, on the other hand—"

"It's staying on." She'd come too far to ruin it now. Her body was primed and ready for him—the one little taste from earlier had only stoked her appetite. "No negotiations."

He rubbed a hand along his jaw, a grin forming. "But I'm a brilliant negotiator."

"I'm sure you're wickedly talented, but I'm not interested. The mask stays on or you can go home and have a cold shower."

He laughed and reached for a bottle of champagne stashed in a small refrigerator that Lainey hadn't noticed. Obviously, Damian had a lot more experience with limos than she did. He expertly eased the cork out of the bottle with a soft pop and poured the liquid into two glasses.

"I can handle a little mystery," he said, passing a flute to her. "But I need you to tell me one thing."

"What's that?" she asked warily.

"You're not married, are you?"

His words were a punch to her heart. It hadn't even occurred to her that he might assume she was married, but it made sense. With his history and her desire to hide her identity, it was a logical conclusion. As much as he acted like he'd moved on, it was clear he still carried the scars from his divorce.

"No, I'm not married," she said softly. "I'm not in a relationship of any kind, I promise."

Damian raked a hand through his dark hair and nodded. "I gave something away, didn't I?"

"Just that you're a guy with morals." She sipped her drink. "But I won't push you for more information."

Damian leaned back against the plush seat, toying with the stem of the champagne flute. Tonight he'd crossed a line that he'd promised himself he wouldn't—at least for a little while—and he wasn't the sort of guy who changed his mind once he'd made a decision.

He was supposed to be off women. Off sex and

head games and all that fuckery, because he needed to concentrate on his work. After finding Jenny and Ben together, he'd screwed his way into oblivion for twelve months straight, and it had done nothing but cause him grief. It hadn't filled the gaping chasm in his chest, nor had it quietened the critical voices in his head. So he'd become very selective about who he let into his bed. And even more selective about who he let into his life.

But then this redhead had bowled him over and flipped everything on its head. Back on the balcony, he'd been powerless to resist her demands for more—and she wouldn't even tell him her name.

"I, uh… I don't do this normally," the redhead said.

"Have a one-night stand?"

"At least not without dinner first." She drained the rest of her champagne. Looking for some Dutch courage, perhaps? He was tempted to remind her that he'd already brought her to orgasm once, so what was there to be nervous about? But he kept his mouth shut.

"We had canapés, so that's dinner covered."

She smiled, but it wasn't seductive or sexy. She seemed…shy. "You know what I mean."

"No judgement," he said, finishing his drink.

Right about now he would have preferred a scotch—two fingers, neat—but this would do. Really, he didn't want *anything* to dull this experience. Something told him that the redhead was special. That this whole crazy thing wasn't going to be regular "good in the moment, but forget it the morning after" sex.

"You don't have to be nervous," he said. "I want this, you want this. All we need to do is settle on a location."

"How about right here?" she whispered. Her cheeks were flushed beneath her mask, the pretty pink extending down her neck and colouring her chest.

"In the car?"

"Why not? As you said, your ticket paid for it."

He stifled a groan as she crossed her legs, the long slit falling open to reveal miles of creamy, pale skin. Knowing she wore nothing but a scrap of lace beneath had made him impossibly hard. He wanted her in his lap, legs spread, moaning his name. Now.

Damian dropped the privacy partition and instructed the driver to circle the botanical garden a few times. With Saturday-night traffic, that should give him ample time to lose himself inside this beautiful, mysterious woman.

Her eyes grew dark, the muscles in her neck working as she swallowed. The low light danced across her skin, highlighting her smooth paleness where the dress exposed the sensual curve of her breasts. Light caught on the shiny silver beads, glimmering like stardust.

His cock hardened even more, straining against the wool of his tuxedo pants. Adjusting himself, he counted to ten in his head. His self-imposed dry spell would work against him if he didn't keep his urges in check. If he was doing this, he wasn't going to blow it in the first five minutes.

"You should know before we go any farther that I'm not going to tell you my name," she said. Her fingertip traced the beading on her thigh. "Is that a problem?"

He clamped his teeth down on his lip and imagined sinking them into her, leaving a perfect indentation on her inner thigh. The idea of such a personal mark on her skin filled him with excitement. How would she react to the sharp sting mixed with all the pleasure he planned to give her?

"It's not how I usually do things," he said, holding out a hand. "But no, it's not a problem."

She slid across the limousine's seat until her thigh touched his, her shallow breathing music to his ears. He grabbed her by the waist and hauled her into his lap so that she straddled him, the slit in her dress riding up even higher to expose the tops of her perfect, creamy thighs.

His cock ached to be inside her. Cupping her head with his hands, he smoothed up her jawline to thread his fingers into her hair. His thumb traced the shell of her ear as he stared at her mouth, watching her lips as her breath stuttered in and out. She sank lower, pressing the heat of her sex against his straining erection, sending sparks of need shooting through him.

"Stop moving," he commanded, whispering into her ear.

The scent of peaches and vanilla invaded his nostrils and filtered through him like a drug. She stilled in his arms and he brought his lips to her jaw, kissing along the gentle angle until he reached her lips. They were plump and juicy.

Slowly, slowly.

Hovering above her lips, he waited to see if she would break. Not a muscle twitched as she waited, compliant. He pressed his mouth to hers, coaxing her lips open so he could taste her fully.

Knotting her hair in his fists, he held her head in place while he devoured her. She moaned into him, the muffled sound awakening every nerve ending in his body. He was going to savour this.

CHAPTER SEVEN

IF KISSING WERE an Olympic sport, Damian would take home gold, silver and bronze. No contest. The man had a mastery over his tongue that was borderline indecent.

He tugged her hair, moving her head into place so he could take what he wanted. How he wanted it. This kind of kiss should have been accompanied by a crash of cymbals or the roar of the ocean. It could have its own soundtrack. But in reality, she was only aware of the slow sizzle of her nerves frying as she slowly melted into him.

"God," he moaned into her ear as he sucked her lobe into his mouth.

Hot breath warmed her skin. He enveloped her, supported her. Held her in place. Only her mouth moved as she kissed him back, her body his to manoeuvre as he saw fit.

He released her hair, smoothing his hands down her neck, his thumb tracing the little hollow at the base of her throat. She could feel her pulse fluttering wildly, and she sucked in a breath, relishing the power he had over her. She willed him to fuck her right here, to tear her underwear to one side like he had on the balcony and release the tension bundled up tight between her legs.

But it seemed Damian had other ideas. Slower ideas. He leaned forward to suck on the skin at her décolletage, his tongue tracing the bones pressing against her skin before he moved down. Safe in his arms, she leaned back to give him the access he needed. He tugged the dress over, revealing her breast and drawing a nipple into his mouth.

He sucked, teeth scraping over the sensitive peak. Was it possible to come from only this? Lainey often orgasmed by her own hands rather than with a partner. The men she slept with thought breasts were more for jiggling and bouncing, but Damian treated hers like the centre of his world. He worshiped them.

She stifled a moan, flooded with the realisation that they were in a car, surrounded by windows. Tinted, thank God, but windows nonetheless. The rush of tires over bitumen flowed through her as Damian nipped at her breast. His tongue circled her before he drew her back into his mouth, the pressure building inside her. Rising until she felt like she'd explode.

"I'm going to get you off again."

"Again?"

"Yes, princess."

The soft words made her tremble, her sex pulsing hotly. Begging. Pleading. She nodded.

"Don't be quiet, okay? I want to hear you this

time." He pressed his lips to her breast as his hand trailed down her stomach and landed on her thigh. "Can you do that for me?"

"Yes."

Hot palms slid up her thighs, pushing the fabric of her dress up to her hips. He moved aside the triangle of lace covering her sex and eased her open with gentle fingers. Probing. Teasing. A gasp caught in her throat.

"You're so fucking wet," he groaned into her ear.

His eyes were dark and smoky, his mouth slack with desire. *She* had done this to him. Feminine power hummed through her body, mixing with the excitement that flamed as he teased her clit with his thumb.

He knew exactly where to press, how hard to push and when to ease back. Orgasm welled within her, threatening to crash over her at any moment. True to his promise, he brought her to the brink and let her hover there, suspended. Weightless. Wanting.

This time he didn't rush her, choosing to toy with her instead. "We're almost there. Just hold it for a little longer."

He traced slow, maddening circles around her clit. She forced her hips not to buck, to let him give her this experience. He controlled the pace and therefore controlled her pleasure. Controlled *her*. Nails bit into her thighs as she resisted the urge to thrust against his hand. She was so close...so very close.

"Take it," he growled.

He applied the last bit of pressure she needed to tip

over, and the air evaporated from her lungs as she fell, fell, fell. She pressed her face into his neck, letting her cries of pleasure vibrate against his skin. Shudders ran through her body, deadening her limbs as she rubbed against his hand until there was nothing left. Until she'd squeezed every last bit of pleasure out.

Lainey wondered if she'd died and gone to some kind of sexual nirvana. She'd been with a few guys who liked the thrill of a public grope—alleyways, nightclubs, taxis. But it had never been her thing.

Until now.

She had a feeling Damian could make her want sex in any possible way, in any possible position. And maybe a few impossible ones, as well. He had a power over her that should have been frightening…only it wasn't. It was the most thrilling, liberating thing she'd ever experienced, and they'd barely scratched the surface.

The sounds and sights of the world cut into her hazy post-sex glow. The honk of horns, tram bells ringing and sirens wailing. Lights flashed in her peripheral vision as they passed the hustle and bustle of the Flinders Street railway station.

Thank God for tinted windows.

"Do you feel like a queen yet?" His hand came to her jaw, tilting her face up to his as he brushed a thumb across the string of black beads shadowing her cheek.

"I'm certainly in the realm of royalty, but I'm not done yet." She leaned forward, endorphins emboldening her, and slid her hand between their bodies.

Through the thin wool of his tuxedo trousers, he was hard. And long. And thick. Perfect. It was like he'd been created with pleasure in mind. Lainey's heart skipped a beat. She was really going to do this—have sex with her best friend's older brother in the back of a limo while he had no idea who she was.

A chord of unrest struck her, sending tiny pulses of worry through her system. The downside of this situation—of her carrying out her mission perfectly—was that he was willing to sleep with her without knowing a thing about her.

Are you really complaining because you're about to get everything *you set out for?*

"Why did you agree to this?" she asked, immediately cursing herself for ruining the mood. "With me?"

"Do you mean because we're strangers?" He removed her hand from his crotch and ran his palms over her shoulders and arms, caressing her. Soothing her. "Because you're beautiful and interesting. Mysterious. Do you want me to try harder to convince you to take off your mask?"

"No." Her gaze dropped. What *did* she want?

"I'm not in the habit of sleeping with anyone who offers, in case that thought is dancing through your mind." He held her hands. "And I can't quite explain it, but I feel like I know you even though I don't. There's something about you that has me quite…"

Lainey looked up, smirking. "Aroused?"

"Yes, but I was going to say 'enraptured.'"

Enraptured. The word summed up everything she'd always wanted to be to him but never was.

Lainey, the crazy magnet. She'd thought once that being wild and impulsive meant she was interesting, but one day she woke up and realised that it exhausted people. But without that persona, who was she? The doubt had plagued her while she made her plans to leave Australia, the little demons in her head telling her to start over. To try her hand at being someone else. Maybe this time she would get it right.

"I don't think I've ever enraptured anyone before," she whispered.

"I sincerely doubt that."

The shocking thing was, he sounded sincere. But he didn't know who was behind the mask, so he couldn't possibly mean it. It was lip service. Superficial. Words to keep the night moving along so he could get what they'd agreed to. Sex.

"You know all the right things to say." She shoved the worries aside and planted her hands against his chest. "Now I guess it's my turn to make you feel good."

If Damian's cock was any harder, he'd be at serious risk of busting the zipper on his trousers. Which would make returning them an interesting experience. Although he already owed Aaron an explanation after he'd quietly demanded that he and Jessie play along with Damian's "fiancée."

Yeah, in the scheme of things, a busted zipper was the least of his problems.

The redhead pulled her dress back into place and shimmied down his body, dropping to her knees at his feet. Between the sight of that smooth porcelain skin, the pressure of her hands on his thighs and her glossy lips parting in anticipation…oh, hell. He'd be carrying this image to the grave.

He'd meant what he said earlier. It *did* feel like he knew the redhead, like they had some existing bond, but that was impossible.

She reached for his zipper and drew it down. Damian shifted his hips so she could pull his pants and jocks down to his ankles. He probably looked ridiculous in a stuffy tuxedo jacket and mask, naked from the waist down, but he wasn't physically able to give a fuck at that point. All that mattered now was the anticipation of having the redhead's lips wrapped around him.

"Do you want it?" She looked up at him, eyes huge from the extreme angle.

She looked doll-like, with lips glistening and open, waiting for him. She hovered, teasing, testing.

"Fuck, yes."

"Then take it."

He growled on hearing his words come from her lips.

She didn't move, she simply opened her mouth and stuck her tongue forward in invitation. He drove between her lips in a single, smooth thrust, and she closed around him tightly. The hot wetness consumed him and stars danced behind his shuttered lids as he gave himself over.

Both hands burrowed into her hair, controlling the bobbing motion of her head. It was pure, unadulterated bliss. With each flick of her tongue, each stroke, he grew closer. Pressure built at the base of his cock.

"Christ," he gasped. "Those sweet lips feel so fucking good."

He tried to pull back but she held him tight, the snug ring of her mouth sending dizzying shock waves through him. He hovered for what felt like eternity before she pulled back at the last minute, leaving him desperate and wanting.

Her lips curved into the most delicious smile he'd ever seen and he hauled her into his lap. "What do you want to do to me?"

Holding her tight with one arm, he leaned forward and fished his wallet out of his pants. He always kept a condom there, though it'd been an eternity since he'd needed one. Lights flickered outside the window, and it looked as though they were rounding the gardens again. He made a mental note to tip the driver generously.

"Tell me," she repeated, plucking the foil from his hands and extracting the rubber. "Exactly what you want."

It was hard to speak with her handling him, slipping the condom over him with sure fingers and her breasts rising and falling against the deep V of her dress. "I want to slide my cock into that tight little pussy of yours and feel you stretch around me. Then I'm going to hold your hips and grind into you until I feel you shake."

She pushed up higher onto her knees and positioned herself over him, holding her dress in her hands. "More."

"I'm going to fuck you until you come so hard that you squeeze every last drop of cum out of me." His voice was a saw now, hard and cutting. So roughed up and dangerous.

"Oh, God." Her breath stuttered in and out as she lowered herself onto him.

The feeling of her tight, wet heat was so sublime, Damian thought he might have been dreaming. But as she sank all the way down and his hands found the curve of her ass, he knew it was real. Nothing that good could come from his mind.

She wrapped her arms around his neck and whispered into his ear, "Make me feel good. Make me forget everything except how you fill me."

There would be no stopping him now. His fingers bit into her sides and he bucked up into her, dragging a groan from her lips. The edge of pleasure was too close already, but he didn't want to hold back. Didn't want to give her slow and sweet and sensual. No, this could only be hard and fast. Passionate. Furious.

He held her tight as she rocked against him, his hips thrusting up to meet her. Her teeth were at his neck, biting and scraping. Tugging. He smoothed a hand down the back of her head, feeling the ribbon holding her mask in place. Then he fisted the lengths of her silky hair and pulled so her face was tilted up to his. Her eyes rolled back and her lips parted, her cries soundless as she hovered at the precipice.

"You're starting to shake." The flutter of the muscles in her sex dragged him closer. "You're so close. Remember what I said. I want you to come around my cock. Take every last drop."

She trembled in his arms, her breaths turning to gasps as orgasm took hold of her. She squeezed him, her hips grinding as she wrung the pleasure from him. Dragging it out of them both until they peaked. He roared into her hair as the release shook him, his cock pulsing inside her.

Thankfully, Damian had a good grip on her, because that was the only thing stopping Lainey from tumbling back onto the floor of the limo. How long had they been driving? Had the driver heard everything going on back here? She reassured herself that if the guy drove limos for the rich and locally famous, he'd probably seen or heard a lot worse.

"Wow," she breathed, her head resting against his shoulder.

"Wow, indeed." His lips brushed her hair. "That was incredible."

If only she could freeze time and stay here forever—in his arms, before the cold reality of what she'd done came crashing down like an avalanche. But it was officially time for Cinderella to turn into a pumpkin. Or something like that.

No doubt Damian would be a gentleman and offer to have the limo drop her home first, which couldn't happen. He'd been to her place a few times. She'd have to give a fake address. Somewhere close enough for her to walk home safely, without giving the game away.

As she moved to climb off his lap, something shifted against her face. The mask slipped, and Lainey's hand flew to the back of her head as shock seized her heart. She felt for the ribbon that held the mask in place, but all she could find were the frayed edges of where it *should* have attached.

Crap! One wrong move and she was about to have the mother of all wardrobe malfunctions.

"Is everything okay?" He reached out for her. But the gesture sent her into panic mode.

He could *not* find out her true identity. She couldn't risk losing his respect, not to mention putting her friendship with Corinna on the line right before she was due to leave the country.

Just hold the damn mask and get the hell out of this car.

"I'm fine," she said, but her voice was tight. "I… I need to go."

Damian glanced out the window. "Right now?"

They were driving down Swanston Street in the heart of the city, not at all close to her apartment. But there were plenty of people around, and she could hail a taxi. Besides, once Damian was gone, she didn't need the mask. And then she'd just be a girl in a dress…a revealing, slightly too tight, impossibly expensive dress.

"Yes, please. Right now." She searched for her clutch but couldn't find it. Shit. Where had she left it?

Her breath came in shallow bursts, her ribs flexing against the tight fabric of the dress, which only served to amplify the panic. She needed her clutch— she wouldn't be able to get back into the house without it. It had her keys, her money and ID. Oh, God, her ID!

If Damian saw it…

She spotted the bag on the floor of the limo. It must have been knocked down in their passionate encounter. She snatched it up and pressed it to her chest as though it were a life jacket.

"We can take you home," he said. "I don't like the idea of dropping you on the side of the road."

"I live in the next block. It was…good timing." Her voice was about as convincing as a politician telling people he had their best interests at heart. She wasn't about to get into acting any time soon. "Please, ask him to stop."

Damian sat still, his large frame seeming even more imposing in the wake of her panic. His lips pressed into a line, but he relented and zipped himself up before pressing the button to lower the privacy partition. A second later the limo pulled over.

"I don't suppose you'll give me your number?" he said. "Even if I promise not to ask your name."

"I can't." She shook her head, tears pricking her eyes.

Why was she being so emotional? This was exactly what she wanted—a night with the perfect man. *Her* perfect man. No consequences…except that she hadn't factored in her stupid heart.

"Thank you," she whispered. She leaned forward

and stole a kiss before pushing the door open and stepping out onto the street, her hand still holding her mask in place.

Lainey waited, her muscles tense and aching, until the limo pulled into the stream of Saturday-night traffic. It disappeared around a corner at the next intersection, and the air flew out of her lungs. Her chest hurt. Her head hurt. The tender spot between her legs hurt, but in the best way possible. Damian had left his mark on her, and she would never be the same.

"Just great," she muttered to herself as she stuck her arm out to hail a taxi. "You're ruined for other men."

As the yellow vehicle pulled over, she opened her purse to dig out her phone. That was when she realised that her grandmother's compact was missing.

CHAPTER EIGHT

DAMIAN SAT BEHIND his desk, turning the compact mirror over in his hands. No matter how hard he tried, he couldn't get that night out his head. It was odd, since he didn't usually mull over a one-night stand. Especially when it was clear up front that it would be a onetime-only thing.

But something about the redhead had got him all tangled up. For the first time in four years, he was thinking about something other than work.

He frowned at the compact. It'd been sitting on the floor of the limo, and he'd almost missed it. Must have fallen out of her bag when they'd knocked it to the floor.

How on earth was he supposed to return the damn thing without a name or phone number? It looked old, possibly a family heirloom. An important item. But there were no distinguishing marks on it—no engravings or product details. Nothing that might help him identify the mysterious masked woman.

Placing it carefully on his desk, he turned to stare out of the huge window that framed the city view like a piece of art. From his level thirty-six office, he could see everything: the tracks running into the Flinders Street railway station, the ribbon of water cutting through the city, the spire at the Arts Centre, and the great stretch of green from the gardens. Ever since he'd walked into his first office job, he'd had his eye on a big corner office just like this one.

It'd taken a few years of slumming it, first working out of his apartment and then—when he'd hired a team—out of a crappy, falling-down building in the inner suburbs north of the city. But his collection of smaller clients had led to some medium-size fish. And those had led to bigger fish. Now he had two blue-chip clients and a healthy list of medium-size businesses that made him very good money.

But he wouldn't be satisfied until he had McPartlin & Co.

"Damian?" His assistant, Leila, poked her head into his office. "I've got a call for you, but you're supposed to be meeting with Corinna in five minutes."

"Who is it?" He swung back around to his desk and raked a hand through his hair. "If it's the tax office again, put them through to Greg. I don't have time—"

"It's Jerry McPartlin," she said. Leila's expression didn't reveal a thing, but Damian had worked with her long enough to detect the hint of judgement in her voice. Since he'd poached her from his ex-boss's company, she knew the history.

"Put him through."

Leila frowned but didn't argue, and a second later the red light on his desk phone flashed. "Hello?"

"Mr. McKnight, how are you?"

"Call me Damian." He reached over to his laptop and pulled up the file he'd been working on before his first meeting with McPartlin. It had everything he knew about the guy and his company—from personal and professional achievements to the AFL team he supported. "I'm well. Did you enjoy the Carmina Ball?"

"I did. The TAFW charity thanks you for your generosity."

The charity were the organisers behind the Carmina Ball. They had a lot of powerful people in their ranks and worked to raise money for various recipients, most notably the Royal Women's Hospital.

"I wasn't aware you were affiliated with them." Damian scanned his file, but nothing about the charity appeared there.

"It hasn't been announced yet, but I'll be joining their board soon." He cleared his throat.

Damian leaned back in his chair. This was going to go one of two ways: either McPartlin had decided to give him a shot at his business, or he was calling to ask for a donation. "So are you calling to tell me you've decided to come across to McKnight Management after all?"

"Let's not get ahead of ourselves," the man replied in what Damian could only imagine was his "stern father" voice. "But I thought we could have dinner."

Damian had to force himself not to fist pump. This

was the opening he'd wanted—a chance to show what he was made of. And really, that was all he needed. Because once Jerry saw Damian on his game, that asshole Ben wouldn't stand a chance of hanging on to McPartlin & Co.

"And by we, I mean including my wife and your lovely fiancée," Jerry added.

Shit. "You really want to put them through the tediousness of a business dinner? I'm not sure about your marriage, but Ariel and I have a no-shop-talk policy at the dinner table."

"It's not a business dinner. It's a social dinner." McPartlin paused. "For now."

"Right."

"And maybe your fiancée could let us know where she got that incredible mask. Sandra is dying to find out." There was a hint of amusement in the older man's voice.

"Of course," Damian said smoothly. No way in hell was he going to pass this opportunity up, and if he couldn't locate the redhead, he'd find a substitute. Because the one thing no one had seen was her face.

Not that anyone else would even come close to her. This woman was the first in years to leave him wanting—wishing. But he knew nothing about her. He had no leads…other than the compact.

"I'll get my assistant to call your office tomorrow and set it up," Jerry said. "I look forward to seeing you both."

The message hung in the air—his fiancée had better be there.

Damian ended the call and stared up at the ceiling. He'd figure something out—he *had* to. For the last four years it had felt like he was moving through quicksand. Work had kept him busy, but the other areas of his life had stalled. One beer-fuelled night a few months ago, he'd seen Jenny and Ben out together. That night he'd packed a suitcase and walked out of the apartment he'd once shared with his ex-wife. He hadn't returned.

Movers had put his things in storage, and he'd been living in a hotel room ever since. He was in limbo. Not wanting to be living in the past, but unable to move forward. If only he could get one back at Jenny and Ben, then he might feel as though he'd levelled the playing field and be able to move on with his life.

He needed a redhead. He wanted *the* redhead.

"Damian?" Leila's voice came through on the intercom. "I've got Corinna here for your lunch date."

"Send her in. I need to finish up an email before we go."

He was tapping away at his computer when his sister walked in. As usual, she looked perfectly fashionable. Her grey eyes—identical in colour to his—were accentuated by a pair of chunky black glasses that would have looked awkward on most people, but looked chic on her.

"Ticktock," she said, dropping down into one of the chairs facing his desk. "We can't be late. I've got a class at two."

"You need to graduate and face the real world sometime, you know."

"I've graduated once already." She grinned. "No one said I couldn't go back for more."

"You're a glutton for punishment."

"There are worse vices in the world than academia. Not all of us are so desperate to become corporate slaves," she teased.

He shook his head, refusing to take the bait. Despite the decade between them, they were as close as a brother and sister could be. Different, yes, but they had a deep bond. Maybe it was because he'd been like another parent to her. He'd cooked her meals, driven her to ballet class and cheered like a maniac as she'd received her bachelor's degree.

But that meant she knew what buttons to push and made a sport out of winding him up. Not today, though. He had bigger fish to fry than letting his sister get under his skin.

"What are you doing with this?" She reached over his desk and picked up the compact.

"Uh…" Close as he and Corinna were, their sex lives were *not* up for discussion. "I need to return it."

"No shit." She flipped the compact open to check her appearance. "Lainey must be having kittens."

Damian blinked. "Excuse me?"

"This is her compact. Well, it belonged to her grandmother, but it's hers now. I've been telling her to put it somewhere safe, but she carries it *everywhere*." She shook her head. "Like a good luck charm. Wait, no…what did she call it?" Corinna snapped her fingers. "A talisman."

Lainey.

There's no way she could have...

A cold fist enveloped his heart and squeezed. But her voice had been different. And her hair had been different.

She's a fucking hairdresser. You don't think she could have dyed her hair?

He forced himself to remain calm...at least on the outside. "You're sure it's hers?"

Corinna looked at him strangely. "Positive. There's a little set of initials in the embroidery, and Lainey has the same initials as her grandmother." She put the compact on the desk and pointed to one of the roses, where a very subtle shift in the colour of the threads revealed the letters *LK*. He'd never have noticed it if she hadn't pointed it out. "She's had this thing since her grandmother passed away years ago. I'd recognise it anywhere."

Fuck. Fuck. *Fuck.*

He couldn't flip out right now, because the last thing he wanted was to explain to his little sister that he'd accidentally screwed her best friend. He needed to play it cool.

"It must have fallen out of her bag last time I gave her a lift." He shrugged. "I found it under the seat of the Audi when I was cleaning it, but I had no idea who it belonged to."

"Because so many women ride in your car." She rolled her eyes. "Do you want me to drop it off to her?"

"No." He shook his head. "I'll return it myself. I'm heading out her way tonight anyway. I should stop in to see her—it's been a while."

"Okay." Corinna looked at him strangely. It wasn't like he'd ever mentioned "dropping in" on Lainey before. But Corinna's stomach rumbled and she huffed. "Can we go now? If I don't eat soon I'm going to turn into Bitchzilla."

"I definitely don't want that." He pushed up from his chair and pocketed the compact.

Tonight he'd call in to see Lainey and confirm if his fears were true—that he'd found the redhead right when he needed her, but that she was definitely someone he shouldn't have slept with.

Lainey stood in her tiny kitchen, cradling a mug of coffee, and quietly tried not to lose her shit. This week had been a complete fucking disaster. First, she'd had *zero* luck in tracking down her grandmother's compact. The limo company had been sweet and checked multiple times for her, but to no avail. Then she'd dropped her phone into a sink full of water and now the damn thing wouldn't turn on. And, like the cherry on top of a giant fuck-you sundae, Imogen's friend refused to accept the masquerade mask back because of the broken strap. Which had meant forking out more money she couldn't afford to buy a broken mask.

Frustration bubbled like lava in her veins. It was karma, for sure. Karma for tricking Damian and keeping secrets from Corinna. And to what end?

"Only the best sex of my entire life," Lainey grumbled.

And not the best sex in the way people tended to

fling those words around. It was *literally* the best. It was the Ferrari of sex. The Chanel of sex. The kind of sex that people scoffed at in romance novels and labelled unrealistic, because nobody could come like that on the first try with a new partner, right?

Wrong.

It was like Damian had been in her head every time she'd reached between her legs in the dead of night, thinking about what she would do with him if only she had the chance. Like he'd saved up all her fantasies and distilled them into one perfect, never-to-be-repeated experience.

And instead of feeling over the moon that she'd gotten exactly what she wanted, she felt bloody miserable, because one taste wasn't enough. Nowhere near it.

She twirled her hair around her finger and startled herself with the bright red hue. She still wasn't used to it. Every time she walked past a mirror she gave herself a fright. But the longer she wore the vibrant colour, the more she liked it.

A knock at the front door snapped Lainey out of her worries and she put her coffee down before going to answer it. "Hello?" she said as she swung the door open.

Time seemed to slow as her brain tried to catch up with what she was seeing. Damian McKnight, standing on her doorstep, looking hot and pissed as hell. He wore a charcoal suit with a white shirt and baby-blue tie, which brought out the subtle blue tones in his grey eyes. But the soft colours did nothing to lessen the impact of his ice-cold stare and the hard set of his jaw. His nostrils flared as his gazed raked over her.

Oh my God, he knows.

"Uh, hi, Damian." She swallowed. "Are you looking for Corinna? She's not here right now."

"I wasn't looking for her," he said. The words squeezed out between his teeth, the razor-sharp edge of his anger palpable in the night air. "I came to see you."

"Oh." She stepped back and held the door, unsure what to say.

Maybe he doesn't know and you're being paranoid. Perhaps he's had a bad day...

He stalked past her and made his way to the kitchen. Everything about his movement screamed agitation—from the stiffness in his shoulders to the fists bunched by his sides. He wasn't saying a word and Lainey had to fight the urge to fill the silence, because she was bound to say the wrong thing.

They were in a nonverbal stand-off. Damian leaned against the counter, stuffing his hands into his pockets, encouraging her eyes to drop down to that general area. Like she needed help in the gawking department. His legs were crossed at the ankles, showing off a pair of expensive black shoes. The position could have easily been mistaken for a relaxed stance, but Lainey wasn't a fool. She knew he was about to strike.

She dropped down into one of her rickety dining chairs and waited, sucking on the inside of her cheek to keep the words from spilling out.

"Haven't you got anything to say to me?" His tone was frigid. "A confession, perhaps?"

Hell, he made Frosty the Snowman look warm and fuzzy.

"Fine," he said after a few beats of silence. "Have it your way."

He pulled one hand out of his pocket and placed her grandmother's compact on the table in front of her. She snatched it up, her breath releasing in a long *whoosh*. Having it back in her possession made the world feel right again, but one thing was now clear: Damian knew *exactly* what she'd done.

"What do you want from me?" she asked, her thumb stroking the embroidery. The worn threads and familiar habit soothed her.

"I want to hear you say it."

The rough, gravelly sound of his voice flooded her with memories of their evening together—it was so similar to the dirty way he'd growled into her ear. A tremor rippled through her, warming her body from the inside out, almost as if anticipating a repeat performance. But that wasn't going to happen. Not since he looked as though he was about to strangle her.

She sucked in a breath. "Why? It won't change things."

"Because I deserve the truth," he said. "You owe me that, at least."

Shit. It shouldn't surprise her that he wasn't going to back down. The man was a bull when he wanted something.

"I snuck into the ball." Her chest constricted, the

enormity of her actions suddenly weighing on her like great big boulders. "I lied about my identity."

"And?"

"I slept with you." Dammit, why did her voice have to fail her now? The words came out jagged and panicky.

"I didn't quite catch that." He folded his arms across his chest, the intimidating breadth of his shoulders casting a shadow over the table.

"I slept with you," she said in a louder, although no more steady, voice.

"You *fooled* me." His eyes were like fire, ready to burn her up until she was nothing but ash. "Why?"

Because I've wanted you ever since I laid eyes on you. I've wanted you in every sense of the word—from the most innocent to the most possessive to the things I could never say aloud.

"I don't know," she lied.

"So I could have been any man, then? You snuck in to have anonymous sex with someone, and I was the guy who happened to end up between your legs?" His jaw ticked.

"No." She shook her head, confused by the hint of jealousy in his voice. Was he bothered that she might have wanted anyone? "It wasn't random."

"Then you targeted me?"

Her chest rose and fell, her breath becoming rapid. What would he say next? Was he disgusted with her? Disgusted with himself? Did his desire lessen now that he knew who Ariel was?

"Yes."

"You've put me in a very hard place, Lainey." He raked a hand through his hair. "A very hard fucking place."

"I'm sorry, I—"

"I don't want your apologies." He sighed.

"Then what *do* you want?"

"Your help."

Lainey raised a brow. "What?"

"We told someone important that you were my fiancée," he said. "Jerry McPartlin. And now he wants me and my nonexistent fiancée to accompany him and his wife to dinner."

"And you want me to pretend to be your fiancée?"

"You did a pretty good job pretending last time." He planted his palms on the table and leaned closer. Next to him, it looked like dollhouse furniture. "Very convincing."

She gulped. "Was I?"

"You screamed in my ear like you were having the time of your life, and I had no idea you were pulling the wool over my eyes." His expression told her nothing. "You got me good."

The feeling was annoyingly mutual. "I didn't hold a gun to your head, Damian. You agreed to the terms."

"If I'd known it was you, I wouldn't have slept with you."

The rejection stung like a thousand blades. "Right."

"So I need you to come to dinner with me next week and play along with your new identity. Okay, *Ariel*?"

"You've got a lot of nerve." She sucked in a shaky

breath, humiliation and anger and frustration roiling in her chest.

"No, *you've* got a lot of nerve. I don't want to do this any more than you do, but here we are." He glowered. "And don't get your knickers in a knot because I said I wouldn't have slept with you if I'd known who you were. It's nothing to do with attraction."

"Then what is it?"

"You're like family." He shook his head as if she were an idiot. "Why would I risk making a mess of that?"

"You don't think it was worth it?" The words popped out before she could think about their consequences.

He looked at her for a long, hard moment, and Lainey seriously wondered if he'd be able to melt her with his stare. "I'm not answering that," he said eventually. "I need you to give me one dinner. Nothing more."

Her heart skipped a beat. "And what do we tell Cori?"

"We don't breathe a word of it to anyone." He pushed up from the table and pinned her with a stare. "Promise me."

"I promise," she whispered.

"Good. I'll send you the details."

Lainey sat, rooted to the chair, as Damian left the apartment. The bang of the door shutting behind him echoed through the quiet space. Then the only thing she could hear was the sound of her heart pounding in her ears.

One more night with Damian, pretending to be his fiancée. She couldn't stop herself from grinning.

CHAPTER NINE

DAMIAN PUMPED HIS arms and legs, gaining speed as his feet pounded the boardwalk planks that lined the Yarra River. No matter how fast he ran or how loud he blasted the music through his earphones, he couldn't get Lainey out of his head.

Knowing the mysterious redhead was in fact his little sister's best friend *should* have put a stop to the dirty dreams. But instead the knowledge fuelled them, gave them life and depth and the sharp snap of reality that had him turned upside down and inside out. Every night was a battle of wills—his carnal self paired with vivid imagination versus his moral core.

It was a terribly one-sided battle.

After his evening run, he was itching to get out of his workout clothes. The soaked cotton clung to his back and chest like a second skin, and he peeled it off quickly. A light ache spread through his muscles, a sign that he'd pushed himself hard today, and he'd need to spend some time on the foam roller to ease out the knots.

He'd been tighter than usual. Stress, his trainer had

said. Lack of stretching, according to the remedial masseuse. Working too hard, his assistant claimed. But he knew it wasn't any of those things.

Desire. He'd felt it burrowing under his skin ever since he'd seen Lainey on Monday night, niggling at him in the quiet portions of the day. In the dead of night. In the dark corners of his dreams.

He shook the thoughts off and stepped under the running water, sighing as the warmth seeped into his muscles. He lathered up, working the bar over his skin. Tonight was going to be an exercise in restraint.

Because sleeping with Lainey again—this time knowing it was her—would only create trouble.

You don't fuck people you care about.

Sex had no place getting mixed up with feelings, that much he knew. But since the Carmina Ball he'd only had thoughts of one woman. And his libido had come back to life like a bear out of hibernation— hungry and desperate for the bounty of springtime.

Just one night.

Temptation rolled around in his mind. Would it be so bad to act on the fantasy that Lainey *was* his fiancée? God, she was gorgeous. Porcelain skin and ruby-rich hair that looked so perfect it should have been natural. Perky breasts that went uninhibited by a bra most of the time. The memory of running his thumbs over her nipples, the stiff little peaks pressing against his touch, rocketed through him.

He was hard as stone remembering it. Without thinking, he reached down and wrapped a soapy hand around his cock. He'd spent every day trying to deny his urges—to deny his fantasies about her—and now all the sexy thoughts had piled up. Testing the heft of his length against his palm, he let the air rush out of his lungs.

The muscles of his ass and thighs clenched as he squeezed himself, sliding his hand up and down slowly. Deliberately.

Bracing his other arm against the cool tile of the shower wall and shutting his eyes, he thrust into his hand. It would never be as good as the real thing, but his flickering reel of fantasies was vivid and bright. He could practically feel the soft wetness of her mouth against his cock, the slippery slide of her tongue and the tight ring of her perfect pink lips.

Orgasm welled within him, pulling his balls up tight against him and making his muscles harden. When he came it was hard, his grunts bouncing off the walls of the shower as he emptied himself, his mind filled with Lainey.

This would have to do. He couldn't let himself get fooled again.

Lainey had expected an email with the details for their dinner date, or whatever the hell she was supposed to call it. Maybe a text. Even a phone call. You know, normal-people communication methods. But Damian didn't do things the way most guys did.

The day after he'd dropped by the house, a parcel had been delivered via courier with a handwritten note.

I'll pick you up at 7:00 p.m. on Friday. Don't open the box until then.

Ever since, she'd been on edge, each night willing sleep to come. But her dreams were no less restless, and the silver box winked at her from across her bedroom. Tonight she'd see him again.

Gripping her towel tight, Lainey skimmed her hand over the subtly embossed pattern, enjoying the feel of the tiny ridges beneath her fingertips. Heart in her throat, she lifted the lid and stared at the layers of frothy, candy-coloured tissue paper.

It crinkled as she opened the edge to reveal a dress. One of those formfitting bandage-type dresses. The straight lines were enhanced by panels of mixed fabric—leather, brushed silk, something reflective and glossy—all in a shade of purple so dark it was nearly black. A fine zipper in gold ran the entire length of the dress from the bust to the hemline.

She steeled herself and glanced at the swing tag, blinking at the neatly printed price label. Surely that last zero wasn't supposed to be there. Lainey's stomach pitched. She could cover a few months of rent with that!

She dropped the dress onto the bed as though it had burned her. In no universe could she accept such a gift. The dress she'd worn to the Carmina Ball had been this expensive, but it had been a loaner and she'd almost ruined it.

Lainey had a thing against charity. The second you accepted it, you admitted that you couldn't take care of yourself. Sure, she might need rescuing from funny situations on occasion, but she had a job that she was damn good at. Opportunities on the horizon. She was her own woman and she paid her own way.

Lainey fingered the fabric. She had to admit Damian had impeccable taste.

Who says he *bought it for you? He probably had an assistant do it for him.*

She bit her lip. Was he testing her? Getting the upper hand back by dictating the terms of their next evening together, dressing her up like a doll so that she would look pretty enough to please his dinner guests?

She stared at her reflection in the vanity mirror as she held the dress up, the gold zipper glinting. Maybe this was exactly what she needed right now—another costume to boost her confidence and help her get what she wanted. In this, no one would look at her like she was lesser. Like she didn't belong on Damian McKnight's arm.

She wriggled into the dress and slipped on a pair of pencil-thin stilettos. Her hair hung in soft waves and her makeup was dark and sultry.

Mask firmly in place.

If he wanted her to act like a smitten fiancée, then she was going to give an Oscar-worthy performance. Without the limitations of her Carmina Ball disguise, she'd be able to tell if he wanted her rather than "Ariel."

She swallowed back her guilt. It felt wrong to be going behind Corinna's back like this, but Damian had set the rules. They weren't to breathe a word of it to anyone. Besides, what harm would one more night do?

Her flight to the UK was booked, and she left in twelve days. It wasn't like they were entering into long-term arrangement, and Lainey had no illusions she possessed that "forever" quality. She was fun—she'd been told it time and time again—but fun didn't make for happily ever after.

One little fling before you leave the country and forget about men altogether.

Before she started her life as a career go-getter—Lainey, the creative. Lainey, the social media guru. She had plans, big ones. Long-term ones. And they didn't include falling in love.

After Damian picked her up, it was all business. He'd briefed her on his plans for signing McPartlin & Co. as a client and gave her an overview of their expansion strategy. Then they agreed on the details of their "relationship." Dating for a year, engaged for two months. They were keeping it quiet because Lainey—*Ariel*—didn't want to deal with the media. No date set for the wedding, but the plan was for a small and private event. Be general but not too vague, avoiding unnecessary details that might make it hard to keep track of the story.

Damian parked beneath the Crown Entertainment complex, and they got out of the car.

"Think you can handle all that?" he asked as they walked toward a set of elevators.

Lainey's high heels made echoing sounds that bounced off the concrete walls. "A few white lies? Sure."

"I guess you *do* have practice."

She jabbed the call button for the elevator. "If you don't want me to apologise, then stop bringing it up. I tried to say I was sorry."

"Apologies are useless." He stared straight ahead, his hand coming to the small of her back as the doors opened. The touch burned through her dress. "You knew exactly what you were doing."

"And I take responsibility for my actions."

"Do you?" He raised a brow. "For as long as I've known you, you've skated through life, leaving mass destruction in your wake."

Her cheeks burned. How was it possible that she could be so attracted to a man who thought she was a hot mess? "Yes, you were incredibly upset after we fucked. I'm sure you'll have mental scars from it."

He was on her in a flash, hands gripping her shoulders as he held her fast. His dark brows knitted into a frown. "Do you have any idea how I felt when I found out it was you?"

She wasn't sure she wanted to know, so she opted for sarcasm instead. "Were you sick to your stomach?"

"I was."

She snorted. "Just what every woman wants to hear."

"I was sick to my stomach because I couldn't get the thought of your body out of my head. I wanted you again. I can't stop thinking about how good it felt to be inside you." His face was inches from hers, his breath puffing across her cheeks. "I was sick over how much I wish you'd come back to my place that night so I could have stripped you down and explored every fucking inch of you."

Her sex throbbed and she squeezed her thighs together, but it did nothing. There would be no satisfaction unless it was him there. All of him. *Only* him.

He continued. "And I can't think about you like that."

"Why? I'm *not* family." She rolled her eyes. "We're not related. We wouldn't be doing anything wrong."

"Yes, we would. Because, as crazy as you are, I don't want to screw things up with us. It's not worth the risk."

She blinked. It was far from the answer that she expected. In her mind, he'd never viewed them as having anything to screw up. "What do you mean, it's not worth the risk?"

"Sex creates tension. I don't like being jealous or disappointed or resentful, and sleeping with someone I care about makes that difficult."

The words her hit like a fist to the chest. "You care about me?"

Damian opened his mouth to respond, but the elevator dinged and the doors slid open. Their private little bubble was gone. "Come on. We don't want to be late."

They walked through the bustling building and approached two large gilt doors. The name of the restaurant wasn't visible from the front, but judging by

the clientele, it seemed to be the kind of place where
if you had to ask then you didn't belong. She knew
it was one of Jerry McPartlin's restaurants, but that
was it. Would he be able to pick her out as a fraud
right away? She was wearing a ridiculously expensive dress, but it might not be enough.

She glanced furtively at the maître d' as they
stepped inside, wishing for a second that Damian
had taken her for a burger and fries instead. But this
wasn't a social catch-up and she was playing a role—
Ariel, Damian's fiancée. Confident, cultured. Definitely *not* the kind of woman who would gate-crash
a society ball.

She swallowed. They'd be able to pick her out like
a cheap knockoff among rows of the real deal.

"Mr. McKnight, what a pleasure." The maître d'
greeted him warmly, her hand gravitating to his arm
as he leaned in and kissed her on the cheek.

"Good to see you, Marcella."

"We've got our best table reserved for you. Mr.
McPartlin and his wife will be joining you shortly."

Marcella's eyes swept over Lainey, curiosity ap-
parent. With a warm smile, she gestured for them to
follow her into the restaurant. Large light fixtures created a twinkling ambience, though the overall effect
was still darkly intimate and sensual. Gold trimmings
tastefully adorned the walls. The vast area housed
small round tables and was lined with booths in dark
wood and rich, plum-coloured velvet.

Lainey followed, still clutching Damian's arm, and
held her breath as they navigated the tight space be-

tween the tables. The last thing she needed was to trip and make a fool of herself. History told her the chances of that happening were as likely as the sun rising tomorrow.

"Relax." Hot breath caressed her skin as Damian whispered into her ear. "You look like you're about to have a heart attack."

"I'm fine," she said tightly, the words sticking in her chest.

They reached a secluded booth at the back of the restaurant. Ornate fabric hung from the ceiling. It looked like a curtain that could be closed for privacy if needed. She ran her hand down the silk, her fingertips grazing over the faint gold embroidery.

"I've got our most experienced server looking after you tonight," Marcella said. "But please reach out to me if you need anything at all."

Lainey's jaw clenched automatically. Marcella looked exactly like the kind of woman Damian *should* be dining with. Articulate. Smooth. Polished. All the things that Lainey had given up hope of mastering.

"Of course."

Damian motioned for Lainey to take a seat and he watched as she slid into the booth awkwardly, the tight fabric of her dress and towering heels making her feel like a circus performer on stilts.

"She's got it for you bad," Lainey observed. "Do you know her?"

"She's a friend." He removed his jacket and hung it on a little hook at the entrance to the booth before sliding into his seat with easy grace. "But I don't want

you thinking about Marcella or anyone else tonight.
I need you on your A game."

Nodding, she wound a strand of hair around one
finger, watching the light catch on the vibrant pig-
ment. Her nerves jangled, and anticipation swirled
through her. With the mask on, she'd felt confident
and in control. But now she was exposed. Maybe Damian was right. Sex with someone you cared about
stirred up a whole mess of emotions, and she was un-
prepared. Woefully so.

But that was no excuse. Lainey might have come
to rely on her friends to bail her out, but she didn't
shy away from her decisions.

You've made your bed—now you have to lie in it.

CHAPTER TEN

THE DINNER PROGRESSED better than Damian had expected, despite the fact that McPartlin steered the conversation away from business every time it came up. However, the older man seemed to have lost his suspicions, mainly thanks to Lainey's brilliant performance.

She'd brought the mask with her and spent a good ten minutes cooing over the design with McPartlin's wife. Every so often, her eyes would flick to Damian and something would pass between them. A ripple of tension, electric with the force of her energy. It was like she wanted to communicate, and though he didn't know exactly what she was thinking, the heat in her expression had his whole body lighting up. Crying out for more.

Crying out for *her.*

The dress he'd bought for her looked incredible. The dark fabric clung to her curves the way his hands had that night. The zip was mostly done up—less than an inch remained open at her bust. It didn't reveal a thing, but it *did* make him think about undoing the dress and tracing the line of the zipper with his tongue.

He didn't know what had gotten into him when he'd bought that dress. He'd only planned to send her the details for the dinner—but he'd walked past the boutique and handed his credit card over before he knew what he was doing.

"I can't believe you've managed to keep the engagement a secret," Jerry's wife, Sandra, said as she raised a gold-trimmed coffee cup to her lips. Her red lipstick left an imprint behind on the white china. "The media is relentless with stuff like that. How did you do it?"

"It hasn't been easy," Lainey said, placing her hand affectionately on Damian's thigh and leaning closer to him. Her expression was as sincere and sweet as apple pie, but under the table her hand inched higher.

She'd been testing his boundaries all night—touching him, planting sweet kisses on his cheek and smiling as she swiped the lipstick mark away with her thumb. Playing the doting fiancée with aplomb.

"Sometimes I feel like I've made the whole thing up," she added with a twinkle in her eye. "I haven't gone to many events with him, but the masquerade ball was the perfect opportunity since I could keep my face covered. We could be together without anyone knowing who I was."

"Sometimes I felt like *I* didn't even know who you were that night," Damian said drily.

Lainey squeezed his thigh, the top of her finger precariously close to where he was doing his best to will away a burgeoning erection. They really needed to stop talking about the ball, because he was struggling to keep the image of Lainey straddling him out of his head. He wrapped his hand around hers, interlacing their fingers and guiding them away from his crotch.

"You'll have to go public at some point," Jerry said. "People talk."

"To be honest, I don't want a life in the spotlight anymore." Damian shrugged. "My company is where I'm focused. I had my fifteen minutes and frankly hated every bloody second of it."

Jerry laughed. "It certainly has its ups and downs. But you do have a face for television, I'll admit that."

"I have a mind for business," Damian corrected. "Television didn't really work out for me. All it did was give me a reputation that I'm not proud of. I'm not fame hungry, and I'm not a womanizer."

He couldn't blame McPartlin entirely for having a low opinion of him. While Damian had come across well on the show, the people who made *Australia's Most Eligible* knew exactly how to interview contestants and edit the footage to tell the story they wanted. They could create villains and heroes out of ordinary men. Or, in his case, men who would do anything to get ahead.

He'd watched half of the first episode the night it aired and had cringed the whole way through. The Damian on that show wasn't him.

"Ah, yes. Well, even those in the industry fall prey to believing what they read." That was as close to an apology as Jerry was ever likely to give, but Damian would take it. "Call me old-fashioned, but I think people today don't value the sanctity of marriage like they used to. Monogamy is a wonderful thing."

"I couldn't agree more," Damian said, reaching for his wine in the hopes of washing the bitter taste from his mouth.

Sandra shot Damian and Lainey a look. "He also thinks today's music is abominable. I'm sure when time machines are invented he'll go back to the '50s and never leave."

"Nothing wrong with having morals," Jerry huffed.

"Well, now that he's on his high horse, it's probably time we leave." Sandra shook her head. "One glass of wine and he gets philosophical."

Damian stifled a laugh. He'd once thought of Jerry McPartlin as intimidating, but it was clear his wife was the one running the show behind the scenes. For some reason, it made him think of Lainey. On the outside she appeared one way—flighty and silly and a little bit crazy—but on the inside she had a fierce determination to go after what she wanted. As much as he disliked her methods, he had to admire her resourcefulness.

"I need to check in with the kitchen," Jerry said, pushing up from the booth. They were seated near a set of doors that led into a high-tech kitchen, which had allowed not only privacy for their dinner but meant Jerry had been able to keep an eye on his staff all night.

"Always working," Sandra commented, shooting Lainey a look. "I suppose Damian is the same."

"Absolutely." She nodded. "He's so dedicated. It's inspiring."

Jerry stuck his hand out to Damian. "Enough with the hard sell already. I'll give you a meeting, but I'm not making any promises. You need to prove you can offer me more than my current firm, which is going to be tough. And at a better price, too."

"It won't be tough." Damian gripped the older man's hand.

"Cocky." Jerry laughed. "There's another problem with young people today."

"All right, grumpy old man," Sandra said as she slid out of the booth behind him, shaking her head. "Time to go."

"There's a VIP bar through the doors over there," Jerry said, pointing. "Marcella has your details if you'd like to go in for a drink. It's very private, so you don't need to worry about people bothering you. But you can stay at the table as long as you like."

"That sounds wonderful, thank you." Lainey smiled, and the room felt as though it'd brightened by a million watts. She stayed seated by Damian's side, blocking the entrance to the booth and waiting until Jerry and Sandra had left the area. "Would you like to get a drink?"

He shouldn't encourage bad decisions—or rather, a repeat of bad decisions. "I should take you home," he said.

"Should?" She raised a brow. "Come on, it's one

drink. You're trying to get this guy's business. It would be rude to decline."

"One drink," he said, giving her a firm look. "And that's it."

Looking far too much like the cat who'd got the cream, she slid out of the booth and headed toward the VIP bar without waiting for him. He stared after her—admiring the curve of her shapely behind through the tight fabric of her dress.

His cock stirred and Damian cursed himself. Normally, it was easy to maintain platonic relationships. In fact, not a single one of the women in his circle had ever made him think twice about his "no sex between friends" rule. Not a single one had even come close to tempting him. But Lainey had him hot and bothered like nothing else.

"Get your head in the game," he said to himself as he followed her.

In the VIP area, the lights were dimmed, a soft glow emanating from the bauble-like chandeliers that hung around the room. The atmosphere held a pleasurable intimacy, perfect for secret sharing and arm touching. He recognised a few of the patrons— a local politician, a TV host he'd met during his time on *Australia's Most Eligible*. No one even looked in their direction. Damian let out a breath.

Lainey headed to the bar and ordered a drink. When it arrived she traced her finger around the rim of the shot glass, the movement slow and languid. It was all too easy to imagine her circling the tip of his cock like that.

"Drink up," he said. "Then I can get you home."

"I meant one drink for *you*." A smile quirked on her lips. "I'm not going to limit myself."

He sighed. "What are you doing?"

"Having a drink with my *fiancé*." Her eyes were piercing, like polished amber. "You invited me—the least you can do is let me enjoy a few drinks."

"We're not having this argument again," he grumbled. "You set these wheels in motion."

"That's the adult version of saying 'you started it.'"

"You *did* start it."

"And you finished it. Three times." She smirked. "Always the overachiever."

A few strands of her hair slipped seductively over one eye. She dipped her pinkie into the shot glass and sucked it clean. The creamy liquid moistened her lips, and Damian felt his mouth run dry. He reached down to adjust himself, finding his cock fully hard and pressing against the zipper of his pants. Christ, how did she manage to do that?

"What are you drinking?" he asked, forcing his mind away from the cleavage peeking out of the top of Lainey's dress.

"Buttery nipple," she replied with eyes wide and purposefully innocent.

Heat flooded his stomach, and he felt his cock clench in response to her full lips wrapping around the shooter's name. And she was doing it on purpose, the devil. She brought the squat glass to her lips and tilted her head back in one liquid movement. Desire blanked out Damian's senses so that all he could see was the ivory column of her neck and the thrust of her breasts as she threw her head back.

"Delicious." She licked her lips. "You should try it."

Stifling the impulse to reach out and pull her into a kiss, Damian pressed his hips against the bar in an attempt to dispel his throbbing hard-on. But all it did was give him the friction he craved and bring him another merciless inch closer to Lainey.

"Are you drunk?" He pulled on his arsenal of big-brother interrogations to force some distance between them.

"Not yet." She grinned, and he could see the tip of her pink tongue between her teeth. "But I could be."

"Behave yourself, Lainey," he warned, though it was more for himself than it was for her.

She rolled her eyes and blinked her long, sooty lashes at him. "Learn to have a little fun, *Damian*."

He had to get out of there. If he watched her down another shooter, he might be tempted to kiss the flavour from her lips, and who knew where that would end up. It was impossible not to notice her body or the sexual energy that swam thick in the air around her.

And now, knowing how sweet she tasted…

"Your brand of fun is a little too over the top for my tastes." He nodded to the bartender so he could order a drink. Something stiff, which seemed fitting. The quicker he downed it, the quicker he could leave. "Why don't you call it a night? I'll get you a cab."

Lainey reached for his wrist, her fingers burning

him as she angled his watch toward her. "It's only gone eleven—the night is young."

"Don't underestimate the value of sleep."

Bloody hell, he sounded like an old man—and compared to her, he was. The extra decade had made him jaded, untrusting. And she was like a ray of fucking sunshine, so happy and optimistic it terrified him.

"I'll sleep when I'm dead," she replied with a wink.

His scotch arrived and Damian snatched it up, sending a good portion of it down his throat in one gulp. The warmth burned pleasantly in his chest.

"I'm leaving soon," she said, suddenly.

"Good," he said. "I want you to text me when you get home, though."

"No, I mean *leaving*. As in, the country." She ordered another drink, this time a glass of champagne. "For good…probably."

"Probably?"

She looked up at him. "Hopefully."

The word socked him in the chest. A few weeks ago he would have sent her off with a wave, wished her the best. But now…things were different. "Why?"

"I've got a job in London, doing social media for a celebrity stylist." She smiled, but not happily. "I felt like it was time for a change of scenery."

"Congratulations." The word stuck in the back of his throat like cactus prickles. He tried to swallow but found a lump there. "Have you told Corinna and Imogen?"

She nodded. "Yeah. I leave the week after next."

He should have been breathing a sigh of relief—

the source of his temptation would soon be gone. But it felt like something had shifted beneath his feet, unsettling him. Throwing him off balance, because what he *should* have felt in no way described the outcry in his head.

"That's not long."

She shook her head. "Nope." When her drink arrived, she raised it to his. "Here's to new beginnings."

"And old friends."

She sipped, a strange expression passing over her face. "Are we friends? I always thought you saw me as some annoying little sister type."

"Those two things aren't mutually exclusive."

She swatted him. "So you *do* think I'm annoying?"

"Well, you are the girl who insisted on telling everyone in which order they could open their Christmas presents."

He remembered it vividly—Lainey as a loud-mouthed ten-year-old telling him and his friends who could go first for their Bad Santa present swap. She hadn't even been invited to the event. But along with Corinna and Imogen, she'd crashed into his family's lounge room and demanded to be part of the festivities.

"Well, I never had any of my own siblings to boss around." She grinned. "You were the next best thing."

"I'll miss you," he said, the words flying out before he could stop them.

She stared at him, her eyes intense and focused. Something flickered there—a hint of emotion? Not positive. But Lainey was as good at hiding her weak points as he was.

"I'll miss you, too," she said.

"You're not planning to come back?"

"Nope." She cocked her head. "So that means you've got two weeks to make use of me as your 'fiancée' before you need to make up an excuse as to why we broke up."

The idea of making use of Lainey in any capacity filled his bloodstream with the snap, crackle and pop of anticipation. Maybe an expiration date would be good for them. Insurance against things getting out of hand, because how much damage could two people do in two weeks?

A lot. Don't kid yourself.

He cleared his throat. "I'm sure I'll be able to come up with some reason for why I screwed our relationship into the ground."

"Maybe you were unable go with the flow and my free-spirited heart couldn't take all that rigidity." She grinned. "Or perhaps you simply couldn't keep up with me in bed."

His nostrils flared. "You should know by now that I can hold my own in that area."

"One night isn't really enough to say for sure." She sucked on her lower lip. "It could have been a fluke."

He leaned closer, dragging in the scent of perfume on her skin mixed with the alcohol on her breath. Her cheeks flushed pink, and her breasts strained against the neckline of her dress as she breathed a little heavier. A little faster.

"It wasn't a fluke, Lainey, and you know it." Against his better judgement, he slipped a hand around her waist and pulled her closer. God, she felt good—so warm and soft and smooth. "I certainly know it."

"That we're good together?" Her lips parted.

"In bed," he clarified.

"Then why won't you let this happen?" She raised a palm to his chest, her fingertips brushing the buttons on his shirt. "Why won't you tell me the truth?"

"About what?"

"How you feel about me." Her eyes were wide, luminous. How on earth had he not recognised them at the ball? Her hunger radiated like a cloud around his head, messing up all the things he should be saying and tying his words into a knot.

"What do you want to know?"

Her lips lifted. "Have you fantasised about being with me?"

Her face was streaked with curiosity. He gripped her hip tightly, fighting back the urge to wedge her against the bar and take her right there on the spot. That mouth was asking to be plundered.

"Yes."

Her hand toyed with the zipper on her dress. "Tell me."

"Why do you want to hear this?"

"Because I've spent a good deal of my life thinking what I felt was one-sided."

She'd never hidden her feelings. Well, not effectively, anyway. When she was young, she'd looked up at him with adoring eyes—the big brother she never had. But as she got older, that adoration turned into something else, something decidedly more adult.

"It's not one-sided, but I knew it couldn't go any-where, so I never acted on it." He brushed a strand of hair over her shoulder, grazing his knuckles along her exposed skin.

"But you're attracted to me."

He lowered his gaze, taking in her long, lean sil-houette, the gentle curves at her waist and the swell of her breasts. "How could I not be? I doubt any straight man could resist you."

"So it's just biological?"

"No." He shook his head. "But that doesn't mean I think we're compatible, either. And regardless, I'm not looking for a relationship."

She stretched up onto her tiptoes and brushed her lips against his ear. "Neither am I."

Aided by her stilettos, she lined her hips up with his. Snaking one arm around his side, she hooked her thumb into the belt loop at his lower back. Claiming him. Being so close to Lainey had made his heart rate skyrocket and his skin hot enough to sear a steak.

"You should go home," he said in a last-ditch ef-fort to maintain his rules. "Come on. We'll get a taxi."

"No." She snuggled closer to him, pressing her face into the base of his neck.

Her perfume wafted up and made it hard to breathe. She smelled like a summer garden, ripe and tempting. Her hair tickled the skin exposed at the collar of his shirt, and he brushed it from her face without thinking.

"Take me back to your place," she said.

It was a bad idea for so many reasons. Lainey was far too important to him for anything to get screwed up. Sure, she was crazy and pushy and reckless, but she'd been part of his life for years. His sister loved her, his parents loved her. As for him... He didn't know how to label it. He felt too old for her, too jaded. But he cared about her, that much was true.

"That's not a good idea," he said.

"What's the big deal? It's just sex. You want it, I want it. Why not have a good time?"

His restraint was like a rubber band pulled too tight—holding on, but threatening to snap at any moment. Excuses swirled in his head, words that encouraged him to have his way with her because it would be temporary, consequence-free. They could hide it until she left—and then they'd be on opposite sides of the world. No chance of awkward run-ins or a slip of the tongue after too many drinks.

"Tell me what you fantasised about," she urged. Her body pressed against his, the gentle back and forth sway of her hips making his cock ache.

Damian gritted his teeth. "Lainey," he warned.

"Do you think I can't handle it?" She narrowed her eyes. "Pretty sure I've proven I can. Or is it that *you're* afraid?"

"Of what?"

"That we might be amazing together...that we're already amazing together? Why does that scare you?"

She was baiting him and doing a damn good job of it. But he couldn't let her know that he *was* scared—

of ruining things with her, with his sister. Vulnerability, however, wasn't something Damian did. Not anymore.

"You really want to know?" he asked.

She nodded.

"I've thought about bringing you to the brink over and over. Holding you back until you beg me to let you come." Images danced in front of his eyes, all the fantasies of her he'd stroked himself to merging together. His control was slipping, dissolving. Turning to dust. "I've thought about fucking you so hard that you forget how to speak. So hard that you can't take a step the next day without remembering how good my cock felt inside you."

Her eyes widened.

"I've thought about that night," he said. "Over and over and over."

"And what do you do while you remember?"

"I think you know," he growled.

A tiny noise escaped her mouth, and already her eyes had taken on a glassy sheen, her movements becoming stiff and jerky. "Take me home," she whispered.

Their conversation was interrupted as the bartender arrived to check in with them. "Can I get you anything else?" The man looked at him expectantly.

Damian downed the rest of his scotch, though the expensive top-shelf liquor tasted like sawdust. "No. I think we're done."

None of his senses would be satiated until he got Lainey to his bedroom. Anticipation bubbled like boiling water, threatening to spill over and burn if left unattended for too long. But waiting was the best part, dragging out the exact moment that he would allow himself—and her—to go someplace new. Someplace terrifying.

The point of no return.

"Have you touched yourself while thinking about me?" She swallowed the remainder of her drink demurely as she waited for him to respond. There was no teasing in her tone now.

"Yes." He swallowed. "Have you?"

She hesitated for a moment. "I have."

"When was the last time?"

"Last night."

He raised a brow.

"Thinking about seeing you again… I was so wound up. I couldn't sleep." Her lashes touched as she closed her eyes for a moment. "But it wasn't the same. I didn't want to come unless you were there with me. I want all those things you said." She spoke slowly, controlling the words.

If he didn't have at least a taste, he was going to burst. Or he'd come quicker than an inexperienced teenager during his first fuck.

"Tell me what you thought about when you were touching yourself," he commanded softly.

She closed her eyes and sighed. "I imagined you taking me to bed, ordering me down to my knees so that I could take you between my lips. I wanted you to tell me what to do, to tell me to suck you until you came in my mouth."

Fuck. Was someone up there trying to test him?

She tilted her face up to his. "I want to try everything with you."

"Fine." The word popped out before he could stop it, warning bells sounding in his head like a cacophony of sirens. "But it's just sex."

"Just sex." She nodded. "Nothing more."

This was a *very* bad idea.

CHAPTER ELEVEN

LAINEY'S HEART THUNDERED like fists beating against drums as Damian led her from the restaurant. This was the moment she'd never dared to hope for—having him, without disguises or trickery. She might have said it was just sex, but her heart knew differently. With him it would always be more, even if she wouldn't admit it aloud.

At least she knew Damian would look after her. He was *exactly* the kind of guy she'd always wanted but never chased. The kind who had his head screwed on properly, who made her feel boneless and tingly. He was the complete package, perfection in man form... well, except for his inability to loosen up. But she was going to help him with that.

His clear eyes searched her face, trying to figure her out as they walked along the boulevard. The night air was balmy against her bare arms and legs, doing little to cool the inferno inside. Focusing on the strength of his arm around her, Lainey put one foot in front of the other and concentrated on keeping her balance in her stilettos.

The world felt like it was spinning around her, due as much to the way reality had rushed back as to the drinks. They rounded the corner and walked through the doors of a fancy hotel. Damian's face was hard, his mouth a slash across his movie star–handsome features. The hotel lobby gleamed, every surface polished and trimmed in gold. A heavy chandelier hung in the centre of the room, sending fractured light in all directions. Her eyes couldn't focus for all the blinding, dazzling finery.

"Why are we here?" she asked.

"You said you wanted to stay the night."

Her stomach dropped. "You're outsourcing me to a hotel?"

Heat crawled up her neck, blooming in her cheeks. So he was happy to fuck her but he wouldn't take her back to his place? Had she really read him that poorly?

He raked a hand through his short, black-brown hair. "I'm taking you home."

"Here?"

"Yes, here." He steered her away from the reception desk and toward a set of gleaming elevators.

"I don't understand."

It didn't make sense. Damian McKnight didn't live in a hotel. She and Corinna had crashed at his apartment plenty of times. He had a glorious view of Southbank and the river, a coffee machine that made the perfect cappuccino, and a couch that was softer than the clouds in heaven. He had a *home*. A real one.

"I live here." He sighed and jabbed the up button with his forefinger. "For the moment."

"And you've been keeping it secret?"

"Not specifically." His voice sounded brittle. "But Corinna knows I'm a private guy, in case you're wondering why she didn't tell you."

Strange. It *definitely* sounded like there was a story there.

An elevator chimed and the doors slid open, beckoning them inside. Mirrored walls reflected her confusion as she searched Damian's face. But he avoided her gaze, pressing the button for the top floor. Her ears popped as they rose higher and higher, the silence only broken by the chime that let them know they'd arrived.

The hallway of the hotel was quiet, and only a few doors dotted the walls. They stopped at the first one and Damian let them in, holding it open for her like he always did. *The perfect gentleman.*

"Whoa."

Melbourne's skyline painted the windows that ran the length of the room. Lights in every colour blinked and bathed everything in a twinkling glow. Damian deposited his key card into a slot by the door and the lights came on.

The suite was larger than most city apartments. It even had a dining table and a study area. Lainey rushed forward and stood at the window, her palms pressed against the glass. The view at his old place had been good, but not as good as this. It felt as though she were suspended in midair, flying above the city and away from her doubts.

"This is amazing." Her breath fogged the glass and she turned to find Damian watching her intently.

"It's temporary," he corrected, and held out a hand to her. "Come on, it's bedtime for you, princess…before you turn into a pumpkin."

He looked as though he belonged in this room, his crisp shirt and inky suit every bit as luxurious as the gold trimmings and soft lighting. She, by comparison, felt awkward in her too-tall heels and too-expensive dress. What *was* she doing here?

He led her to the bedroom, and her breath caught in her throat. Damian loosened the collar of his shirt, revealing a smattering of dark hair. She knew for a fact that it sprinkled the rest of him, too—decorating him in all the right places.

She wondered how it might feel to have the weight of him pressing her into the bed. To straddle him and watch his face contort with pleasure in the moonlight. She reached for him. Her movements were clumsy, nerves stripping away her motor skills.

He watched her, eyes wide and pupils blacker than night, while he drew a long breath and squared his shoulders. Lainey knew the signs well; she'd seen them that first time she'd tried to kiss him, three years ago. His first instinct had been to respond, but as quick as it had started, he'd pulled back. Now he looked the same, with tension bunching his muscles. She would not let Damian run, not when she'd finally found a way to make the sadness in her heart seem conquerable. Under his gentle exploration she felt renewed, alive. Safe.

"I promised myself I'd never go here," he said.

The conflict in his voice called to her, and she wanted to kiss him until he forgot how to speak. "Too late."

"It's not too late for me to do the right thing." He pulled back, breaking free of her greedy hands. "I can go back outside and we can wake up tomorrow morning and act like this never happened."

"As if you'd be able to forget me," she teased.

"I said *act* like it never happened...not forget." He shook his head, dark hair gleaming in the moonlight. "Unfortunately, I'll never forget."

She drew her zip down slowly, the sound cutting through the quiet room. His eyes tracked the movement, swallowing up every inch of bare skin as it was revealed. And she was bare all the way down.

"Christ." His muttered curse sent anticipation zinging through her as she dropped the dress to the floor and stepped out of her heels. "You were sitting there naked under that dress the whole evening?"

"Uh-huh." She stepped forward and reached for him, brazenly drawing her fingers along his fly. "Now strip."

This time there was no argument. He disposed of his suit jacket and popped the buttons on his shirt one by one. His bare torso looked paler in the glow of the city lights, but each muscle was defined to perfection. He was a powerful, virile, intoxicating man.

She slid her hand over his thigh and felt the muscle

twitch in response. Emboldened, she ventured farther by brushing her fingertips over his straining erection, eliciting a gasp from him. His hand shot down, fingers wrapping around her wrist as he yanked her hand away.

"Lainey," he growled. "Wait—"

She cut off his words by pulling his face down and kissing him. Hot, hard, wet. She explored him ruthlessly, revelling in the taste of him. A guttural moan reverberated in his throat, and he ground against her.

Balancing on her tiptoes, she fused their bodies together. Sighing into him, she thrust her hands into his hair and tugged. Hard. The buckle of his belt dug into her belly, and his mouth seared a trail from her lips to her collarbone, each kiss hungrier than the last. She had to have him, had to have every glorious inch of him.

The moment when the fight left his body filled her with a roar of power so loud and forceful it shook her to the bone. She had him *exactly* how she wanted him—without disguises. Without pretence. His shoulders dropped and his kiss intensified. It was as if the temperature in the room shot up a hundred degrees, and the air around them sizzled and popped. His fingers bit into her hips, teeth nipping at her skin. He was marking her, claiming her with his touch.

Then she was being lifted, wrapping her legs around him while he spun her. Two steps and her back met with the glass of the hotel window. It was cold on her bare skin while the front of her burned brightly, flames licking and growing with each stroke of his tongue. She traced the corded muscles in his neck, her fingertips smoothing over his Adam's apple.

Stubble scratched at her skin as he devoured her with gentle nips of his teeth. She wanted to see the marks, to see the evidence of his desire. A shiver shot down her spine, deepening the ache between her legs.

"Put me down," she whispered. "I want to touch you."

"Not yet."

He carried her to the bed and dropped her onto the mattress, settling on his knees and pressing his face between her legs. He kissed her there, swirling his tongue over her clit and wrenching a cry from her.

"You're so fucking perfect." He trailed kisses along the length of her heated sex, each one sending shock waves through her.

What had he done to deserve this incredible woman in his bed? He traced the sensitive curve of her inner thigh, chuckling as she bucked against him. He was going to draw it out, make her beg. He'd been hungry for so long, and she was a hot meal, a cold beverage, the light at the end of the tunnel. Every fucking cliché in the book…but it felt real. Special.

She writhed on the bed as he took his time getting to every line of her body. He drew his tongue up to flick over the sensitive bud of her clit.

Nails bit into his skin, delicious pain slicing through the fog in his head. He grabbed her hands and brought them together, easily encircling both wrists in one strong grip. He held her steady, making sure she couldn't move to touch him while he pleasured her. Her hips lifted from the bed, pressing shamelessly against his face.

"Patience," he said, swirling his tongue against her mercilessly. Each stroke was gentle, designed to wind her up but hold orgasm out of reach.

"You're a cruel man, Damian." She threw her head back. "I can't take it."

"You *will* take it." His voice came out edgy, raw.

Familiar desire crowded his senses. He was losing his grip. Restraint was slipping through his fingers with each groan and under-the-breath curse out of Lainey's mouth. She was a firework, ready to explode and burn them both.

He wanted to be burned. Tonight, he wanted it more than the air in his lungs.

"Damian, please." She lifted her head and her hazel eyes caught his attention. "I'm not too shameless to beg."

She laughed then, the breathy sound sending heat coursing through him. Her wrists tugged in his one-handed grip, but he held on, restraining her. That action alone had him hard beyond anything he'd experienced in a long time. And those smudgy, smoky, needy eyes...fuck.

He bit back the words swirling in his head. The filthy things he longed to say to her. But Lainey was someone he cared for...and you didn't speak to princesses the way he wanted to speak right now.

"Please." She drew the word out, long and agonisingly delicious. "I need to come."

He plundered her without warning, so that her gasp rang in his ears for what felt like hours. He dipped a finger into her core, delighting in the way her muscles clenched around him. Ecstasy could be found right here, with a woman on the brink of an orgasm he controlled. She hovered at the precipice, body grinding and writhing and desperate for release, while he dangled her over the edge.

"You taste so sweet," he murmured against her, breathing her in and savouring every second of it. "You're so soft, so perfect."

He drew the tight bud of her clit between his lips. The soft murmur of eagerness at the back of her throat swelled into a crescendo of pleasure as she shattered. He held her wrists tight, her muscles flexing as she came apart with his name on her lips.

He only released her when the last waves of her orgasm subsided and she lay sprawled on the bed, skin damp and glowing in the moonlight. Her eyelids fluttered and he crawled up on the bed to hold her. He pressed a kiss to her lips and she curled into him.

"I always knew you'd be good at that." Her hand traced the flat circle of his nipple, fingernail scraping gently over the sensitive peak. "You've got a good mouth for giving head."

He chuckled. "That so?"

"Yep." Her hand dipped lower, cupping the bulge

of his ready-to-burst cock. "Full lips, stubble for the right amount of friction…"

Her fingers wrapped around him, stroking the length of him through the thin material of his suit pants.

"I think we need to relieve you of these," she said, a coy smile on her sweet lips.

He couldn't strip down quick enough; if he didn't have her now he'd burst. Need thrummed in his veins, urging him to move quicker. He threw open the drawer next to the bed to grope for the little foil packets. It'd been so long he wasn't sure he had any left, but when his fingers brushed the telltale crinkled material he sighed with relief. He sheathed himself and then came back to the bed, his hands pressing down on either side of her head. The mattress shifted, accommodating his weight as he nudged her legs apart with his knee.

"I've been thinking about this nonstop since that night," he said.

She shot him a smug look. "Even when you were telling me it was a mistake?"

"Just because I was trying to do the right thing doesn't mean I wasn't thinking about burying myself inside you." He lowered his head to hers.

"And now?" Her lashes touched, lips parted and glistening in the lamplight.

"And now…if you keep talking I'm going to have to gag you, because I don't want to wait a second longer."

Her mouth opened as if she wanted to say something more, but it snapped shut a second later.

"Wise choice, princess," he growled, slipping his hand between them to find her slick and needy. "Brace yourself. You've got me all worked up."

He pushed into her, burying himself deep. When her hands came to his chest he grabbed her wrists with one hand, forcing them above her head. She whimpered, her sex clenching around his cock as he thrust.

Fantasy didn't even begin to compare to reality. On the nights since the ball, when he thought of her, his mind hadn't been able to accurately conjure how tight and hot and perfect she was in real life. She was made for him, a perfect fit. And that one crazy night in the limo was nothing compared to this.

Because this wasn't just about her tight body or sexy, smoky stare. It was *her*...all of her.

Her hips bucked against his, her arms straining against his grip. "Keep your hands above your head," he growled. "Don't make me stop."

He released her and her hands immediately fisted in the duvet, her knuckles white. "Please don't stop."

"Tell me what you want, Lainey."

"I..." She stopped to moan as his hand came between them and found her clit. "Oh, my God. I want to come again."

He bent his head down to her ear. "You want to come again, greedy girl?"

"Yes," she panted, her head lolling back and forth. "I want to come against your hand."

Sweet fucking hell.

As if it wasn't enough that she'd been so perfectly responsive, the desperation in her voice as she told him how she wanted to come was…everything.

He applied pressure to her clit, working his hand in circular motions until he felt her clench on his cock, as shock waves raced through her, her body trembling beneath his. It was all he could take to hold on a second longer before he felt his balls draw up and he tumbled into the abyss after her.

Rolling onto his back, he took Lainey with him. Her face pressed into the curve of his neck, her breath hot against his already flaming skin. She murmured his name and an incoherent pleasure sound that washed over him like a warm blanket.

When his strength returned, he pushed up, cradling her in his arms. He carried her to the bathroom and set her down, keeping an arm around her waist as he flicked on the large tub's tap.

"Let's get cleaned up," he whispered in her ear.

She nodded mutely, her body sagging into him, and her arms tucked up against his chest. In the mirror he could see the faint pink marks where he'd gripped her hard. By morning, evidence of their night together would be gone, with only memories to keep him going.

He tested the temperature and helped her into the bath, disposing of the condom before following her and drawing her back to his chest. Her head rested against him, the length of her hair swirling in the water as the tap ran. Tracing circles on the inside of her thigh, his mind whirred with tomorrow's possible outcomes.

"Stop thinking," she said, grabbing his hand and interlacing her fingers with his. "Everything is going to be fine."

CHAPTER TWELVE

DAMIAN WOKE THE next morning feeling as though he'd been transported to Eden. Rolling over, he reached for Lainey but found an empty mattress. Rubbing the heel of his hand into his eyes, he sat up. Clinking sounds came from the kitchenette, and he got up and pulled on a pair of pants.

"Rise and shine," Lainey sang as he walked into the main area of the suite, the chime in her voice making him smile.

He raked a hand through his hair. It'd been a while since he'd felt this exhausted in the morning. Sleep deprived in the best way possible, but still...what he needed was a nice strong cup of—

"Coffee?" Lainey appeared in front of him, holding out a steaming mug.

"You're an angel." He reached for the cup.

It was an apt description, considering how she looked right now. Endless legs extended out from the bottom of a soft white T-shirt—*his* T-shirt—which barely covered her. Her breasts were unrestrained beneath the fabric, nipples peaked and tantalising.

He frowned. "You're still here."

"Did you expect me to bail?" She dropped down onto the coffee table in front of him, one long leg draped over the other.

He'd hoped in the light of day she'd be easier to resist, that without the tight dress and heels he might stand a chance. But no...this was a hell of a lot worse.

Karma was a cruel and enticing bitch.

"I wasn't sure you'd want to stay."

She cocked her head. "Do you want me to go?"

Ah, this old dance. It was one he avoided with most women by getting the fuck out of Dodge before it was necessary to communicate. But that wasn't how he wanted to handle things with her.

"I didn't say that."

"You look sleepy." She grinned when he rolled his eyes. "Drink up."

He shook his head and sipped his coffee. "Same old bossy Lainey."

"I have a proposition for you." She kicked her feet up onto the couch next to him so that all he could see was miles of peaches-and-cream skin. "I'm going to stay here, and if by the time midnight comes around tomorrow you don't want to sleep with me again, I'll go and I won't ever mention it again."

"Is this some kind of messed-up Cinderella sex thing?" He watched her over the rim of his cup.

She poked her tongue out at him. "More like Beauty and the Beast."

"Charming."

"So we're on?" She put her hands on his shoulders and leaned forward so the ends of her hair tickled his bare chest and stomach. "No offence, but my money's on me."

Her lips hovered close to his, her knees nudging his thighs apart. His blood fizzed and raced as though she'd hooked him up to an electrical outlet. Each breath was an effort, desire crushing him from the inside out. Holy hell, if the girl could do that from mere proximity...

She winked and released him. "I'm having a shower—feel free to join me."

Then she sashayed off as though it was her place, not his. Hair swung behind her like a band of scarlet silk, brushing the hem of the T-shirt. Her arrogance should have grated on him, but he found it oddly charming and comforting. She made no attempt to adjust herself to him, no attempt at false niceties or trying to please him. Since his stint on television, he'd noticed how people acted differently around him, and it pissed him off to no end.

The sound of the shower snagged his attention. It was tempting to join her...oh, so tempting. But he had to get his head straight and figure out just how long he was going to play her game before one of them got burned.

Water poured over Lainey, warm and soothing. Last night she'd seen another side of Damian. It had been every bit as perfect as she'd hoped for—hot sex, no head games. He'd wrapped her up in his arms and held her all night.

Unease settled in her stomach. She was already trying to convince him to give her another night—another hit. She was an addict, craving her next fix, chasing satiation that would never come. She turned her face against the spray and chuckled. She must be crazy after all. Who else would chase a man so hard knowing it wouldn't go anywhere?

The door to the bathroom hadn't budged an inch. Hmm, so he wasn't taking the bait. She rinsed the conditioner from her hair and turned off the water. Fluffy white towels hung from the gleaming silver rack—one of the perks of living in a hotel. Her brows crinkled. Why *was* he living here? He'd sold a perfectly good apartment to live in a hotel that probably cost as much per night as she earned from a month of hairdressing.

It was definitely something Corinna would usually have told her. The fact she hadn't meant this wasn't simply a change of scenery for him.

She gave her body a quick wipe-down and then wandered, stark naked, into his bedroom contemplating what to wear. Her dress from last night had barely been appropriate for an evening on the town let alone for the bright sunshine of the morning after…but it wasn't like she had much choice.

She tugged on the stretchy dress and riffled through Damian's wardrobe, plucking out a clean white shirt. She slipped it on, rolled up the sleeves and located the emergency ballet flats in her hand-bag. There she also found her touch-up makeup palette. It wasn't perfect, but at least she wouldn't look like something the cat had dragged in.

"Going through my clothes again?"

Lainey whipped around. "Thought I'd make an effort to look respectable. So, what are the plans for today?"

He folded his arms across his chest. "I don't think we should be playing games like this."

He was probably right. The little bundle of doubts was already growing, the voice in her head warning her that she was going to be flying to London with tears in her eyes. But if the end was nigh, then she'd go out all guns blazing. What was the point of small regret? Might as well go hard.

"We made a deal, so I'm staying. You can ship me off at midnight if you want. But until then…you're stuck with me."

"I don't remember agreeing to that." He closed the distance between them in two long-legged strides. "Besides, you're too young for me—"

"Too young? I'm almost twenty-five."

"You should go for someone your own age…"

"Ugh." She rolled her eyes and flipped her hair over one shoulder, fully aware of just how much that action supported his argument. "You're not that old, Damian, but you sure do act like you're a hundred sometimes."

"See?"

"No, I don't see. Like I said, I'm sticking around all day, so you can stay here and argue with me—which would be pointless, because I'll outlast you—or you can take me for a coffee. A real one."

"What if I told you straight up I don't want to sleep with you again?" He pulled her closer, staring down at her in what might have been an attempt to intimidate. Instead it made her body burn, need gnawing at her insides.

"I'd call bullshit."

A smile twitched on his mouth. "Fine. Coffee it is. It's probably safer to have you out there than in here."

She grinned. "You'd like to think that, wouldn't you?"

The day was already hot. Sunshine filtered through the trees lining the café strip, sending dancing speckles of light across their table. They'd found a quiet spot on the courtyard of a café, private enough for them to talk. Because Lainey had questions.

Swiping at her croissant, she tore off one end and stuffed it into her mouth. "So what's the deal with the hotel room?"

He sighed. "It's a long story."

"We've got all day."

He stared at his coffee cup for a moment before looking up with a blank expression. "I couldn't stand to be in the apartment any longer."

Lainey had known Jenny well enough to know she and Damian were completely and utterly wrong for each other, though she'd never said it to his face. They'd gotten married at twenty-four—a conservative ceremony without passion—and cracks started showing less than a year in. Jenny had been over-bearing. Her family was even worse. Then one day the marriage ended suddenly and Damian had never spoken of his ex-wife again.

Not even to explain *why* the marriage broke down. To this day it was a mystery.

"Why?" Lainey asked. "What changed?"

"Nothing, that's exactly the point. I thought I'd have gotten my shit together, moved on…something."

"But you have moved on." She sipped her coffee, shielding her eyes from the sun with her hand. "You're like a completely different person now. Well, like how you used to be before."

He shook his head. "I'm not."

"Yes, you are. You were so uptight when you were with her. You were tense all the time. It was like you were always trying to force something when she was around, like you were trying to be something else." She sighed. "You weren't yourself."

Damian quirked a brow. "Really?"

"Yes." She swatted him across the table. "And don't look at me like that. I can say insightful shit from time to time."

"'Insightful shit'?"

He was mocking her, the bastard. "I know what I'm talking about." She crossed her arms, self-conscious for the first time.

She could be stark naked in front of him, in the throes of orgasm, and be confident. In control. But the second it came down to the personal stuff—she couldn't have felt more exposed.

"No need to get defensive. I'm quite partial to insightful shit." His eyes swept over her, skimming the neckline of last night's dress and her bare skin exposed between the open lapels of his shirt. Was he remembering the way he felt when she lowered the zipper? When she'd bared herself to him?

She leaned forward. "Why do you think you haven't changed?"

"This is a bit heavy for breakfast conversation, don't you think?" He raked a hand through his dark hair and the front sprang forward rebelliously.

"We might be eating breakfast, but it's hardly early. Besides, I get the impression it would be heavy conversation for you no matter what time it was."

"I prefer to keep things light. Sue me."

He attempted a look of nonchalance, but his gaze flicked over her. Hot and intense. Sunlight streamed down over their table, shifting so that the trees around them no longer provided protection. Lainey slipped the white shirt off and bundled it on top of her handbag. The sunshine felt good on her bare arms.

"I could tempt you to get heavy." She smirked. "I convinced you to sleep with me, after all."

Damian's Adam's apple bobbed and his gaze narrowed, two flintlike eyes challenging her. "Once."

"Twice," she corrected.

"The first time doesn't count."

"Then I'll do it again." She shrugged. "You're just buying time now."

"I'm not buying anything."

"Yet." She jabbed a finger in his direction. "I've got all day."

"You're going to need all weekend at the rate you're eating that croissant." He nodded to the barely touched pastry sitting in front of her.

"Would you prefer it if I stuffed the whole thing in my mouth at once?" She sucked on her lower lip, stifling a smile. "That's not very ladylike, is it?"

Damian's serious expression broke, his eyes crinkling at the corners, and he laughed, low and throaty. She needed to see him laugh more often.

"Since when are *you* ladylike?"

"Good point." She grinned.

Her phone vibrated against the glass table, Corinna's picture flashing up on the screen. Lainey's smile faded; she didn't want to talk to her best friend right now. Guilt twinged low in her gut.

Ugh, why did they have to be related? Or rather, why couldn't she only want the physical with Damian? Why did she need more than their memory-obliterating night in bed? There was nothing wrong with some serious, scream-the-roof-off fucking. She knew that. Dirty, impolite sex was her favourite kind.

But with him…it was always going to be more.

"What's with the expression?" he asked. "You look like you're plotting a murder."

Lainey wrinkled her nose. "Plotting a murder, huh? How would you know what that looks like?"

"I picked you up from that freak's house one time, remember? I'm pretty sure if I'd walked past a mirror my face would have looked exactly like that."

"Which freak?" She rolled her eyes. "There have been so many."

"Why *do* you always have to date idiots?" He drained the last of his coffee and tilted his face up to the sun. "Aren't there any normal guys left in Australia for you to choose from?"

"Despite what you might think, I don't always get my pick of the litter." She rolled her shoulders back, stretching her arms in front of her. "Besides, you rejected me."

He pressed his lips into a flat line.

Yeah, and it has nothing to do with Corinna or Jenny. It's because you're not forever material. You're not good enough for him.

She would ban all doubts until the weekend was over. She would get Damian back into bed and she *would* forget about the fact that she was leaving everything she knew in under two weeks, all because she couldn't have the man she wanted with all her heart.

CHAPTER THIRTEEN

GIVEN THE EVENTS of last night, Damian didn't want to heap his personal problems on Lainey. Because that would take them squarely away from casual sex and into…not-so-casual sex. Either that or he was still so ashamed about the divorce that he couldn't bear to talk to anyone about it. Not even her. His family and Aaron knew what'd happened, but they'd all been sworn to secrecy.

It was *his* business. His private shame that he hadn't been able to keep his wife happy.

"So you sold the apartment because you think you haven't gotten over the divorce?" she pressed as they exited the café.

"Well, it was never going to be *my* place," he said, slipping on a pair of sunglasses to shield himself from Lainey's intense stare. "No matter how much time passed, I could still feel her there."

"And you want to move on?" She looked at him with earnest eyes, glimmering with hope. That was exactly what he *didn't* want from her.

He knew Lainey had a crush on him when they

were growing up, because she was as subtle as a sledgehammer. Problem was, as time went on, he grew more and more attracted to the chaotic girl with the heart of gold. It pained him to admit, but she'd been in and out of his fantasies since his divorce.

He shoved the conflict aside, making a silent promise that it would be a single indiscretion. An isolated incident—well, except for the night of the ball, since that time had been out of his control—and that he would send her home…later.

"I'm ready to move on, yes." He paused. "But I'm past that whole fairy-tale bullshit thing now. Moving on does not mean looking for someone else to marry."

She considered that for a moment, her head bobbing slowly. He wondered if she might want further details. And he was ready to shut her down if she did.

"Sounds like you made the right decision to move…but a hotel? Really?" She frowned, her brows crinkling. "That's not a home. You don't even have a proper kitchen."

"I want to find the right place, and I'm not going to rush things this time." With the apartment or with a woman. "And the hotel owner is a client."

Trees lined the patch of greenery that ran parallel to the river. Chairs dotted the edge, most of them occupied by couples and families enjoying the summer warmth. Arm in arm, Damian and Lainey would have looked like any other couple. Their footsteps dropped in perfect unison, a synchronicity that only developed after years of being around one another.

"I can help you move on, you know." Her voice

turned coy, a sly smile spreading across her lips. "I want to help."

"I don't need your help." Against his better judgement, he reached out and touched her hair; the long red waves looked as though they belonged on a mermaid. On a mythical creature. Not on this crazy, impulsive woman.

"But you might *want* my help." She stepped closer.

"I don't." The words stuck, and Damian had to force them out. "Want" was too high up in his vocabulary when it came to Lainey.

"Why are you so uptight?" she asked, tilting her head. A cool breeze swept past and ruffled her hair, sending the vibrant waves across her shoulders. "What are you trying so hard to repress that you've turned into this…"

"Curmudgeon?" he offered.

"I don't even know what that is, but it sounds about right." She threw her hands in the air and huffed.

"It means killjoy."

"Yes, killjoy. That's *exactly* the word I was looking for." She grabbed him by the shoulders and shook him. "I am going to make you have some fun."

He wrapped his hands around her wrists and lowered them, hanging on to her for a moment longer than necessary.

"Why don't we find you an apartment?" she said.

Now, that wasn't a bad idea. A few property inspections would keep them away from his hotel room, and talking about kitchen layouts was a hell of a lot easier than talking about his divorce...or why Lainey was such a risk to him.

"Fine, apartment hunting it is."

Half an hour later they were following a brisk-mannered real estate agent into a penthouse apartment in Southbank. Turned out she was a huge fan of *Australia's Most Eligible* and the name Damian McKnight meant she dropped her other appointments quicker than a hot potato.

"This apartment was previously owned by a CEO who lived in Sydney and needed a base in Melbourne," the agent said as she held the door open for them. "As you can see, it looks brand-new."

"It would have to be for three million," Damian said under his breath.

Lainey stifled a smile, standing close to him as he inspected the kitchen fittings. Marble benchtops gleamed as sunlight poured in from floor-to-ceiling windows. The kitchen was sizable, and all the fittings looked as though they'd never been used. He could correct that.

"Couldn't you see us in this kitchen, Damian?" Lainey asked, loud enough so the agent could hear.

Her hazel eyes sparkled with mischief, hands knotted in front of her as she beamed at him. He shot her a look. What the hell did she think she was doing?

"We could make such a mess in this great big space." She smiled at the agent, wrapping an arm around Damian and giving him an affectionate squeeze. "You know, I do most of the cooking at home."

The agent arched a brow, her gaze sweeping over Lainey as one might inspect something on the bottom of their shoe. Lainey's dress left miles of long, creamy leg on display, and her smudgy, sexy eye makeup was more suited to midnight than midday, but that didn't give anyone the right to judge her.

"I'm sure you'll find all the fittings here to be of the highest quality, Mr. McKnight," the agent said, continuing to move through the room. "It would be a shame for a man like you to waste your money on something not up to standard."

He didn't miss the quick flick of the agent's eyes toward Lainey. Luckily, she was too busy trailing her hand along the edge of the marble countertop and looking out at the view to take notice. Damian's jaw clenched.

"I make it a point never to waste my time on things that don't meet my standards. My fiancée knows I have very particular tastes."

Lainey's head shot up and she grinned at him. "Yes, dear. You are *very* particular."

The agent looked at him in disbelief, her mouth popping open for a second before she snapped it shut and walked toward the lounge room. "The living area is open plan, as you can see, but there is an additional space for recreation. If you follow me through here..."

"Recreation, hmm?" Lainey tugged him after the agent. "That's very important. We should make sure it will fit all our recreation...equipment."

Damian stifled a laugh. The agent's face had turned the deep shade of a tomato, and she scurried along in her heels, changing direction and gesturing for them to follow her to the bathroom. He knew it was wrong to pay the agent back for being a bitch… but it had been so long since he'd had any fun.

It was true. All work and no play had made him a very dull man indeed.

"You can see the bathroom is very generous. There's a double shower and a deep tub. The towel racks are heated. You can control them with the switches here," she babbled, unable to look either of them in the eye.

"Double shower would be great," Lainey said in mock seriousness. "The last thing we want is to break the glass like we did at that holiday house."

Damian smothered his laughter with a cough. "Yes, that was rather expensive."

"We had fun, though, didn't we?" She walked past him and brushed her hand brazenly along his crotch.

Unfortunately for Damian, while the words were joking, her touch had a very real effect on him. As she wandered out of the bathroom, she shook her hair out so that it tumbled unrestrained down her back, and his pants tightened considerably. That merest touch, a graze of her fingertips, had made him rock hard in an instant.

He followed Lainey into the master bedroom, watching her walk. The hem of her dress was borderline indecent, but she had such fantastic legs it would have been a crime for them to be hidden away. He was thrust into a memory. Last night. His lips on her, those smooth, perfect thighs parted for him. Only him.

"Is this a king-size bed?" Lainey asked the agent, who looked more than a little annoyed that she'd ended up dealing with his fiancée.

"Of course it is, ma'am." The agent nodded stiffly.

"Please, don't call me ma'am," Lainey replied with a saccharine smile. "I'm way too young for that."

If Damian had a drink he would have choked on it. Perhaps his earlier assumption that Lainey hadn't noticed the older woman's attitude toward her was incorrect. She seemed to be enjoying herself far too much.

Stop it, he mouthed at her.

As the agent made her way into the enormous walk-in closet, Damian grabbed Lainey by the arm. He brought his lips close enough to her ear that he brushed her earlobe as he spoke. "If there's a report on some gossip site tomorrow that I enjoy dating young women, I'm going to blame you."

She laughed, the deep, throaty sound sending whatever blood was left in his brain straight down to his cock. Turning her head, she batted her eyelashes at him. The bronzy smudges of makeup around her pale eyes wound him up even more. He wanted those eyes looking up at him while he drove into her mouth. He wanted to see her blink as he pressed between those lips. Pushing as far as he could, seeing how much she could take.

Stop that shit. Right. Now.

"I haven't even told her how you like me to dress up as a schoolgirl yet," she teased.

"Liar." He squeezed her arm, pulling her tight against him. "Don't. You. Dare."

"Or what?" She blinked at him. "You'll punish me?"

He wanted to press her up against the bedroom wall and kiss her until her knees gave out. "Don't tempt me."

She stepped out of his grip, following the agent into the closet. Bending forward, she pretended to inspect the finish of the built-in shelving. Her hem rose higher, inching toward the pleasures that lay beneath. Knowing there was nothing to cover her under the dress was bad enough. Waiting to see if he'd catch a glimpse was pure torture. He turned, facing the endless stretch of glass that revealed Melbourne's skyline and adjusted himself. His cock strained against his jeans, and he had nothing with which to hide himself. Nothing to conceal that Lainey had far more of a hold over him than he wanted.

Her laughter rang in his ears as she materialised beside him. Up close, the smell of his soap on her skin stoked his desire. The heat of her body pressing gently against his tested his barriers.

"Enjoying the view?" she asked.

"It is a fantastic one," the agent chimed in. "People pay a lot for a view like this."

Lainey cupped her hand over her mouth, trying not to laugh. Damian watched her from the corner of his eye. Pink had spread across her cheeks, her red-lacquered nails shimmering against porcelain skin.

"I do appreciate the view," he said, not daring to look at her directly.

"Can't you imagine waking up to it every morning? Going to sleep with it every night." Lainey pressed on, linking her arm through his. "Watching the moon."

He snorted and tried it cover it with another cough. He needed to get out. The longer he imagined what it would be like to see Lainey standing stark naked against the window, the creamy flesh of her backside presented for him, the harder it was going to be to compose himself.

"So what do you say, Damian? Do you want to pay for the view?" Her hand squeezed his bicep.

"I need to think about it." He nodded at the agent. "Thanks for showing us around. We have to talk before we can make a decision."

"There are several other properties I could show you." The agent hurried over to him, plucking a business card from a fancy silver holder in her leather notebook. "We could make a time—"

"I'll get in contact if I'm interested in seeing more." He cut off her sales pitch and made his way to the front door, Lainey in tow.

"Oh, you're interested," Lainey whispered as they left the apartment and headed toward the elevator. "I can tell."

"What makes you say that?"

"Apart from the fact that your jeans look a little… snug?"

"A little?"

She laughed. "A lot."

By the time they made it out to the street, Damian

had managed to calm himself down. Okay, so he was attracted to Lainey. He knew that already. She was fun, hot and confident. What wasn't to like? Any guy would have the same reaction.

It wasn't a big deal. He'd simply sit her down when they got back to his hotel and tell her that he cared about her too much to have her as anything but a friend. He'd made a mistake, but he wouldn't let it get between them. In the meantime, he had to deal with this crazy, pent-up sexual frustration. But screwing his way out of it wasn't going to work…that much was damn clear.

"It's boiling," Lainey moaned as they wandered back to the river. She fanned herself with one hand. "Let's get ice cream."

"You haven't had lunch yet."

"Thanks for the nutritional lecture, *Dad.*" She swatted him. "I can have ice cream for lunch if I want."

He shrugged. Ice cream actually sounded like the perfect antidote to his overheated state. They strolled along the tree-lined boulevard as he tried to settle his mind. Everything about this situation screamed potential disaster, but he couldn't force himself to put an end to it.

Does it matter? She's leaving the country soon. You have an end date.

But that was the thing with Lainey—she never played by the rules. Never stuck to the plan. He needed her to know why he couldn't engage in anything serious.

Perhaps he should tell her the truth about his divorce. Then she might understand his actions better.

Even thinking about it brought heat to his face that made his skin prickle and his chest feel tight. It'd been four years, and still the shame burned as brightly as it had the day he'd caught Jenny and Ben. All he'd ever wanted was for his marriage to fulfil him and his wife, and he had believed that Jenny wanted that, too. Unfortunately, when tested, it was clear that what Jenny had really wanted was for him to sacrifice his career ambitions to spend more time with her...or else she'd get revenge.

The sun beat down on them as they walked. Lainey had ditched the white shirt again, and perspiration beaded along her bare arms and her chest. The dress clung to her like a second skin.

"Why so serious?" Lainey asked, tilting her head up to him and shielding her eyes.

"I was thinking about the apartment," he lied, fishing his sunglasses out of his pocket and handing them to Lainey.

She slipped them on, the large mirror-like lenses obscuring her eyes. "Why were you frowning, then?"

"It's a big decision." He spotted a café with an ice cream counter up ahead. "I'm weighing up my options."

"What are your must-haves? The things that you absolutely won't compromise on."

"You mean aside from a great view?" He smirked. "Space for a big desk, a bigger bedroom."

"What else?"

"Somewhere to relax and zone out. A place where I can think."

Lainey shook her head. "You think too much."

"I thought we were talking about the apartment." They joined the long, snaking line for ice cream.

"We are, but the apartment is a representation of you." Lainey pushed the sunglasses on top of her head.

"How so?"

"You want a big desk because you're ambitious and your business is a huge part of your life. You want a big bedroom because you have a lot of shit to deal with and you need somewhere to be yourself."

His shoulders rose, fingers balled into fists by his side. "What does the bedroom have to do with being myself?"

"Because you hide things when you're out in the world. When you're at home, it's just you. You can stop pretending." She smiled. "Maybe that's why you moved into a hotel without finding a new place first. You know you don't want to be who you were with Jenny, but you haven't figured out what the next step looks like."

He gaped at her, unsure whether to laugh off her comments or immediately drag her back to his hotel room. Perhaps he too was guilty of underestimating Lainey; she obviously saw deep into him. She knew him far better than his ex-wife ever did.

"You really *do* say some insightful shit."

She grinned. "I sure do."

As they approached the ice cream counter, Lainey's attention locked firmly on the rainbow selection of treats. She tapped a finger to her lip.

"What flavour are you having, Damian? I'm buying."

"No, you're not." He pulled out his wallet, but she slapped his hand.

"I said *I'm* buying. You paid for this ridiculous dress and left the tags on. So I know you should be broke by now." She winked at him.

"Vanilla bean," he replied. "Single scoop."

Lainey turned to the woman behind the counter. "I'll have two waffle cones, single scoops. One rocky road and one caramel crunch."

"No vanilla then?" Why did she even bother asking?

"You're not a vanilla guy, Damian. I know that much."

"Does this mean we're done with the amateur psychology hour?" he asked drily, accepting the two cones from the woman behind the counter as Lainey paid. "Which one do you want?"

They walked away from the café, and she contemplated her options before plucking the caramel cone from him. Her tongued darted out to capture the ice cream and she sighed. "So. Damn. Good."

Lainey and Damian walked along Southbank, past the busker in the Super Mario costume playing guitar and the chalk artist drawing people's faces on the ground. They ate in silence, mouths working quickly before the sun melted the ice cream onto their hands.

Damian tucked in to his rocky road with enthusiasm. And he'd wanted vanilla? She smiled to herself, remembering the way he'd hardened when she'd touched him during the apartment inspection. Vanilla was for guys with unsteady hands and fumbling fingers, and Damian wasn't one of those guys.

They came to a stop at a bench that overlooked the aging beauty of the Flinders Street station. It rose up, magnificent and unusual among the sleeker office towers in Melbourne's skyline. The old building had character. Though weathered, it held a certain charm in its mustard-coloured facade and iconic green dome. There was beauty in its age and history, the scars of decades making it even lovelier than it would have been when brand-new.

"Are you shocked that I know you so well?" Lainey asked, still looking out over the water.

"You don't know me as well as you think. One accurate psychoanalysis doesn't change that."

"But you *do* hide from the world," she pressed.

She had an inkling that he covered up his true self for the same reason she relied on zany antics and a crap ton of eyeliner—for fear that people wouldn't like what was underneath. She fought against a memory of being dumped because she'd dropped out of school.

Not like she had a choice. School had been slowly stifling her—trying to stuff her into a box that was too small and too dark. She couldn't seem to follow the rules that were designed for kids with long attention spans and the ability to make sense of numbers. Lainey's skills lay in areas that weren't marked on paper.

Nowhere in the curriculum had she been praised for her ability to defuse a tense situation or cheer someone up. The fact that she could instinctively tell what colours would look good on people meant nothing. Not even in art class could her creativity flourish because, even there, the rules had stifled her.

After that, she'd learned to be someone else. She wore short skirts and acted out. She attracted guys who didn't care that she still counted on her fingers, guys who were only after one thing. All so she could call the shots. So she never again had to face the humiliation of being dumped because she wasn't good enough for the longterm.

"It's something I have to do," he replied, concentrating on his ice cream. It was torture watching his tongue and lips devour the treat with surgical efficiency.

"Why?"

He shook his head, and a smile tugged at the corner of his lips. "Things have happened that make me wary of putting myself out there."

"I haven't done anything to criticise the way you are."

"Other than calling me boring or stodgy, you mean?" He took a bite out of his waffle cone. "What about that one time you said I was the Antichrist of fun?"

Lainey's cheeks burned. "Okay, so maybe I said those things. But it's because…"

"I'm no fun?"

"You are when you allow yourself a little breathing space." She shrugged. "You always act like it's your job to protect everyone around you."

"It is," he said without hesitation.

"No, it's not. I appreciate all the times you've bailed me out, I really do." Lainey finished off her ice cream and put her hand on Damian's knee. "But you need to stop worrying about everyone else and start worrying about yourself. Or else you'll be a... what did you call yourself?"

"A curmudgeon?"

"Yeah, that."

"I'm never going to stop worrying about you." He turned and Lainey got the full force of his Blue Steel stare.

Could he see right into her soul? Did he know that she was a woman who wanted to run away from her life? Away from the fear that she would forever be in one-sided love with him?

The feeling slammed her in the chest with the force of a freight truck. Sure, she'd thought it so many times before—that she had a thing for Damian. An insatiable, unending schoolgirl crush on her best friend's handsome older brother. Harmless...until it wasn't.

Love. How was it possible to love someone who didn't love you back? It was cruel that humans had been designed that way. She tugged on the hem of her dress, paranoid that her fear and devastation were shining out of her.

"You don't need to cover it up, Lainey. I saw it all

last night." His words hitched, his voice rough and ragged around the edges.

Was he referring to her body or to the unwieldy mix of terror and desire warring inside her?

She swallowed, her hand lifting to cup the side of his face. A light stubble showed along his jaw, and her thumb swiped against his lip to capture a tiny smear of chocolate. The only movement he made was the quickening of his breath, hot against her hand. He kissed the pad of her thumb, then caught her hand and pressed his lips to the inside of her wrist.

Darkness engulfed his eyes, grey irises shrinking until there was nothing but a mere rim of it around two bottomless black holes. "I hide because I'm afraid that I might hurt you."

Lainey puffed out her chest, chin tilted up to him. "I won't let you hurt me."

She wouldn't. *Couldn't.* Because if she allowed him to crash through the careful fence she'd set up around this encounter, he'd railroad her heart until it broke for good. This was just sex—fulfilment of a fantasy. And that was all it could ever be.

CHAPTER FOURTEEN

LAINEY SAT IN the middle of her room, surrounded by boxes. They were labelled—not with descriptions of the items inside, but with names. Imogen. Corinna. Mum. She'd divided her not-so-worldly possessions into two piles—keep and discard. The keep pile was further sorted into boxes for the person who would appreciate the items most.

For some reason, it reminded Lainey of a will reading. She was going, and all that would be left of her was an insanely large shoe collection and her childhood set of *The Powerpuff Girls* on VHS. She should have appointed an executor for her stuff. That way she could whisk herself off to London and leave someone else to deal with it all.

She popped the lid on a dusty plastic tub that was packed to the brim with memories—her grade-six polo top with all the signatures of her friends written in puffy fabric pens. A tattered-looking friendship bracelet with the silver beads containing the initials *C*, *L* and *I*. A photo album wrapped in a *My Little Pony* pillow case, the cover dusted with pink glitter from some stickers that had shed sparkling particles all over the place.

She flipped it open and grinned. The first page had three almost identical shots of her, Corinna and Imogen in some awful-looking hipster jeans with super-wide belts, strappy metallic halter tops and silver lipstick. In each photo, one of the girls was making a silly face while the other two laughed. They'd never been able to get a shot with the three of them looking good all at once. The Goof Balls, her mother had called them.

Lainey flipped through the album, her heart sinking with each page. Through every up and down, these girls had been by her side. Through every terrible hair phase, every eyebrow-plucking accident, every celebrity obsession and every tearstained heartbreak, Imogen and Corinna were woven into her life. There was no part of Lainey's history that didn't include them.

She flipped to the last page and found a loose photo. The image caused her heart to stutter. Scrawled in pen was a date ten years ago. New Year's Day. Lainey had still had her natural mousy hair then, and it hung down to her waist without a kink. On her head she wore a plastic tiara with "Happy New Year" in glittering letters. She held a giant slice of watermelon.

But her eyes weren't on the camera or the food. They looked up to Damian. He'd been in his early twenties then, muscular and tanned. Yet his face was soft and free, his grey eyes crinkled with laughter. The emotional scars hadn't yet turned his jaw to stone.

The memory shot through her like a firework—she'd gone to Corinna's place to celebrate with the McKnights. They'd bought a watermelon and hacked it into pieces. Damian had been a little hungover and thus, not paying attention, he'd bit into the melon and a pip had shot across the table and hit Imogen square between the eyes. They'd laughed until tears had streamed down their faces.

Lainey didn't remember staring at Damian, but the open adoration was captured brilliantly in the photo. On the back, she'd written "if only" and the date in purple ink.

If only he hadn't let Jenny ruin his heart. If only they hadn't wasted the years since his divorce with her being too chicken to tell him how she really felt and him looking at her as though she was too young, when she wasn't.

"Is it safe to come in?" Corinna asked as she and Imogen poked their heads into Lainey's room. "Are we likely to die under an avalanche of stilettos?"

"It's safe." Lainey found her throat tight, the words struggling to slip past the lump blocking her airway.

"What's wrong?" Corinna's smile disappeared as she kicked off her work pumps and dropped down cross-legged next to Lainey.

"Ah, you're taking a trip down memory lane." Imogen bent down and picked up the album, flipping through and laughing. "Oh, God, Corinna. What were you thinking with that hair?"

She turned the album around and Corinna cringed. "I look like a skunk with those chunky highlights."

Lainey swallowed against the lump in her throat and forced herself to smile at Imogen. "So, what's the latest with your sister and Dan?"

"Ugh, don't ask." Imogen shook her head. Ever since the ball, she'd been quiet about her mission. "It's a mess."

Corinna raised a brow. "Why?"

"I had to get someone else involved. A guy from work who knows him." Her cheeks flushed pink. "But I feel like he's trying to hold it over my head. I never should have asked him to help me."

The pink flush turned darker still, and Lainey had a feeling there was a whole lot more to the story than that. But there was one thing she knew about Imogen—she'd only talk when she was ready.

Pushing her for information never went down well.

"Are you taking all your albums with you?" Corinna asked, turning to Lainey.

"I can't." She shook her head. "No space."

Imogen patted her arm. "I can babysit them for you."

"I thought I'd be okay with all this." To her horror, hot tears pooled in Lainey's eyes and no amount of furious blinking would chase them away. They splashed onto her cheeks and rolled toward her chin. "Am I making a huge mistake?"

"No." Corinna put an arm around her shoulders. "Not if you're going *to* London rather than running *from* Melbourne."

"How can I do one without the other? It's two sides of the same coin." She sniffed and swiped the back of her hand along her cheek.

"If you're going somewhere, it's a forward-momentum thing—you're chasing an opportunity or an experience. If you're simply leaving Australia because you want to run away, and London is where you happen to land, then it's not moving forward, is it?"

"Do you remember that day?" Lainey asked, scooting over so the three of them could sit together in the small space between her bed and her closet.

"Yeah, I feel like I still have an indent in my head from that damn pip," Imogen said drily.

Corinna laughed. "How could we forget it? We had that slip-and-slide thing in the backyard and you decided to take the cat on it."

"I did!" A heartfelt laugh burst from Lainey's lips. "She scratched the hell out of my arm and wouldn't go near me for months. We were so stupid back then."

"We?" Imogen asked in mock indignation. "Speak for yourself. I *knew* that was a bad idea at the time and told you as much. You were too busy trying to impress Damian and his mates."

"Not his mates," she said with a sigh. Worry coiled tight inside her. She'd never seriously admitted to her feelings in front of Corinna before. All the previous times she'd covered the words with bluster and exaggeration. "Just him."

Guilt gnawed at her. This was the only thing she'd ever kept from Corinna, without at least having the intention to fess up at a later date. How had she thought it possible to walk away and act like none of it ever happened—the ball, the weekend with Damian? Dragging Imogen into her lies?

"I told him once to stay away from you," Corinna said, wrapping an arm around Lainey's shoulder. "After the divorce. I said if he ruined our friendship I'd never forgive him."

"You did?"

"Yeah. I don't think he took me too seriously. But I saw how he looked at you then." Corinna sighed. "And I was jealous. You two always had this spark and I knew you had a crush on him and, well, *all* the boys had crushes on you. Ever since we were teenagers."

"They did not." She rolled her eyes.

"That summer you dyed your hair white-blond and got your braces off, I don't think I've ever been more jealous. *Everyone* looked at you, and I was still in my ugly duckling phase." She adjusted the glasses on her nose. "After he split with Jenny, I caught Damian watching you when you came over for a swim, and I was furious. It was so stupid, but I wanted someone to look at me like that. In hindsight, I wish he'd ended up with you instead of her."

"I slept with him." Lainey blurted the words out, unable to carry the guilt a second longer. Then the fear of knowing she'd crossed a line whipped through her—confessions could never be taken back.

Corinna sat up straighter and snapped her head toward Lainey. "When?"

Imogen bit down on her lip, her eyes swinging

back and forth between her friends. But she didn't say a word.

"Recently." Lainey swallowed. "I had it in my head that since I was leaving…"

"It might be your last chance?"

"Yeah."

Corinna's expression was hard to read, but she didn't look as though she were about to fly off the handle. "And you're still leaving?"

"Sex doesn't change that." She waited for Corinna to make her usual fake-disgusted reaction, but her best friend was uncharacteristically serious.

"Is that all it was?"

"Do you even want to be talking about this? It's your brother." The tears prickled her eyes again, and Lainey tipped her face upward, begging them to stop. "I know how you feel about something happening between us. I thought you'd be furious."

"It's not like I didn't see it coming a mile away." She brushed her thumb over the photo. "Honestly, I thought one of you would have caved earlier than this."

"You're really not mad at me?" Lainey asked.

Corinna shook her head. "Like I said, there's always been something between you two. And I know now that sometimes you can't help who you fall for. Joe wasn't the man I thought I would end up with."

"You seem so perfect together."

"We are, but I had it in my head that I'd marry some ambitious lawyer type. A career guy who wanted the great Aussie dream." She shrugged. "Instead I met a schoolteacher who wants to move to the beach and have a veggie garden and a couple of chickens…and I couldn't be happier."

"You two are total opposites." A strange expression washed over Imogen's face. "It's nice. Balanced."

The pressure slowly eased out of Lainey's chest. Keeping secrets from Corinna had been weighing her down, forcing the spring out of her step. But worse still was the growing fear that running away to London would do nothing to ease the ache in her chest. That no matter how many continents and oceans she put between them, Lainey would never be over Damian.

"He didn't treat you badly, did he?" Corinna picked at a frayed patch on Lainey's carpet. "I know he doesn't mean to be a dick, but he hasn't been himself the last few years. Sometimes I feel like I don't even recognise him anymore."

"He was great," she said. "Treated me like I was special even though I'm not."

"Don't say that." Imogen frowned. "You *are* special."

"Not enough, apparently. If I was that great, he would have wanted me for more than a weekend."

Corinna looked at her pointedly. "Did you ask him for more?"

Lainey bit down on the inside of her cheek. "Well, no… I mean, he knew I was leaving. There was never any discussion about it."

"Then why would he suggest more if he knew you had this amazing career opportunity overseas?"

Lainey wanted to scream at her friends to stop giving her hope—to stop inviting her to leave room for that tiny, blissful bubble of what-if, because it wasn't going to happen. If she went to Damian now, heart on her sleeve, he would break her. Ruin her.

Aren't you already broken? If you were fine, you wouldn't be sitting on the floor crying over an old photograph. Whether you tell him or not, you'll never escape how you feel.

"What if I go to him and it *was* just sex?" she whispered.

"Does that change anything in the grand scheme of things?" Corinna cocked her head. "I mean, if you're leaving anyway, isn't it better to know?"

"Cori's right," Imogen said. "You can't get closure if you're still wondering how he really feels."

Lainey had no idea which option she preferred. Leaving now without seeing Damian would mean a lifetime of asking herself what might've happened. But if she went to him and he rejected her...

Would she be able to move on? She honestly didn't know.

Lainey caught a glimpse of herself in the full-length mirror across the room. Her hair gleamed like scarlet silk, rich and bold and vibrant. It wasn't a colour one wore to blend into the background, even though it had been intended as a disguise. Pushing up from the floor, Lainey went to her handbag and pulled out the compact.

"That damn compact." Corinna laughed and shook her head. "How did I not figure it out then?"

This one little item had brought her back to Damian after that fateful night. What might've happened if she'd never dropped it in the limo? They might not have spent last weekend together. She might never have known that they were perfect together. That they were perfectly balanced. She ran her fingertip over the *LK* embroidered in the flowers.

Do it.

The voice in her head started as a whisper and grew until the words pounded in time with the rush of blood in her veins.

Do it. Do it. Do it.

She sucked in a breath. Her friends were right—there *was* a difference between going to England and leaving Australia. She didn't want her doubts following her to a new country. It was confession time.

She loved Damian McKnight and had for as long as she could remember. And now she was going to tell him.

Damian couldn't stop the grin spreading across his face as victory pumped through his veins. He'd been staring at the email for a full five minutes, revelling in the knowledge that he'd won. Jerry McPartlin was going to sign as a client.

They'd met earlier this week, and Damian had pulled out all the stops. He'd worked with his top consultant, the two of them dazzling McPartlin & Co. with all the ways they could improve the business—cost-cutting through efficient processes, giving him more money without the need to lay off employees,

not to mention implementing a talent-retention pro-
gram to lower their turnover rate, thus keeping the
people they'd invested in. The pitch had required
back-to-back all-nighters, meaning Damian had slept
on the couch in his office. But it'd been worth it.

Victory.

He couldn't wait until his phone lit up with Ben's
number. His old boss would be livid. Served him
right—karma was going to bite that bastard where
it hurt.

The strange thing was, Damian's natural instinct
made him want to call Lainey, to share his good news
with her, to thank her for her role in helping him
land the biggest deal of his career. Because his hard
work would have meant nothing without her by his
side—she'd charmed the McPartlins, played the perfect sweet and sassy balance to his harder personal-
ity. All without judging him, without making him feel
bad for chasing his career with an insatiable hunger.

She got him. Understood him. Had never once
tried to change him.

He scrolled through the contact list on his phone
until he found her name. But before he had a chance
to call her, his intercom buzzed.

"Damian, your 4:00 p.m. conference call has been
pushed. Stacy said they needed another twenty-four
hours to get the information you've requested for the
case study." The sound of fingernails clicking against
a keyboard filled the pause. "And Lainey Kline is
here to see you, but she doesn't have an appointment."

"That's okay." His heart thumped. "Send her in."

A second later, Lainey walked through the doors like the very embodiment of his desires. She always sent a jolt of electricity to his libido, and the feeling had only grown stronger since their weekend together.

"Hey," she said, her hands fiddling with the end of her long red ponytail. Today she looked different. There was no dramatic makeup, no fitted clothing or sky-high heels—none of her usual attention-grabbing tactics, in fact. "I hope I'm not interrupting."

"You're always welcome here," he said, gesturing for her to have a seat. "I was going to call you, anyway."

"You were?" A smile ghosted across her lips.

"I signed Jerry McPartlin." He clapped his hands together and leaned back in his chair. "And I owe you a celebratory drink. Couldn't have done it without you."

"I'm sure that's not true." She ran her hands over the floaty hem of her white cotton dress. The stark contrast with her flame-red hair made her look like a firework against a black-and-white background—like she was the only bit of colour he could see.

"My first meeting with the man was a disaster." He laughed. "If it wasn't for you going along with the whole fake-fiancée thing, I doubt he would have given me a second chance."

"I'm glad I could help. I know he's an important client."

"He is." For some reason he felt a little less victorious than he had the moment the email had popped into his inbox—would Lainey still be happy she helped if he told her the full story? "He was my old boss's client."

Her brows dipped into a frown, as if she was unsure of the significance of that detail.

"Jenny was having an affair with him. My boss... ex-boss." He cleared his throat, startled by the rush of anger that resurfaced fresh and raw. How many years would pass before those feelings stopped? "I found them. Together."

She blinked. "I had no idea."

"I didn't want you to know. I didn't want *anyone* to know." He sucked in a breath. "The worst thing was that it started as a revenge screw. She didn't want me starting my own business because it would mean even longer hours and she thought I neglected her enough as it was. She told me if I was a good husband then she never would have had to go elsewhere."

"That's a load of bullshit." She pursed her lips. "And it certainly doesn't excuse an affair."

"Well, my boss was a bastard, and when I resigned he told me I'd never make it to the big leagues, that I'd never be on his level. He'd hired me to be his gofer and nothing more."

"So you stole his client?" Lainey asked.

"His favourite client."

She picked at the embroidery curving around the hem of her dress. "Why are you telling me this?"

"You were involved." He shrugged. "I thought you had a right to know."

"If you thought that, you would have mentioned it

before I got involved." She looked up. "Do you still love her?"

"Jenny?" He reeled. "Fuck, no. Not after what she did."

"But you're still clinging to her." Her expression was soft and sad and not at all what he'd expected. "This whole revenge thing says you're not over what happened. You said yourself it's the reason you couldn't stay in the apartment. She's still part of your life even if you don't want her to be."

Damian's mind whirred. He knew he didn't love Jenny anymore. *That* was a certainty. But her betrayal haunted his every move. Mocked his every step toward success, telling him it would never be enough. *He* would never be enough. Not until he proved that they'd been wrong to doubt him.

That was why McPartlin was so important. Landing this client was the key to him being able to move on, because it was proof he'd become successful... wasn't it?

Is that really the kind of success you want?

"She's not part of my life anymore," he gritted out.

Lainey shook her head. "But you haven't had a real relationship since."

"Because I don't want one." He swallowed. "I told you that."

"Why did that change?" Frustration gave her voice an edge, subtle enough that most people wouldn't hear it. But he did, because he knew her. "Was it due to her cheating, or something else?"

"I was sick of having to take sides between her and my career. I didn't want to be in that position again."

"Bullshit." She folded her arms.

"You think I'm lying?" He planted his hands on his desk, his fingers curling against the polished wood.

"I think you're deluding yourself. If what you said was true, you would have broken things off with her *before* you found her cheating. Or if you knew things were going to end anyway, you wouldn't still be pissed about it years later."

Her ability to see right through his facade was borderline terrifying. No one had ever done that before. He was damn good at projecting the image he wanted, cultivating a persona that kept the real him safely tucked away, protected from harm. But Lainey was smashing through his defensive walls with a battering ram.

"And I'm supposed to take relationship advice from you?" He regretted the words the second they slipped out in a misguided need for self-defence.

Way to go, dickhead. You've attacked the person whose opinion you care about.

The realisation chilled him. He *did* care about Lainey's opinion. A lot. Why else would he be airing his dirty laundry to her? He didn't want to lie.

"The thing is, I know where my issues come from. I'm not in denial about who I am." Her voice wobbled, and that unsteady sound was like a knife through his heart. "The reason I date all those idiots is because I know I can't have the man I truly want."

The blood stilled in Damian's veins. She could

only say one of two things next, and he didn't want to hear either of them. Because if she loved someone else, he wasn't sure he could stand it. And if she loved him...

Shit. How could he have let this get so out of control? He never should have taken her back to his place the night of the dinner. It was the stupid strength of lust and desire that had allowed him to ignore his own rules. No other woman had gotten to him after Jenny. He'd only ever satisfied physical need. Sure, he'd felt attracted to other women. But that was it. Something he could swallow down as easily as a pill.

But with Lainey his control slipped away like water through his fingers.

Her lip trembled. "Aren't you going to ask me?"

She'd led him to a fork in the path, forcing him to stop and look ahead. Forcing him to decide. When she left his office, something would be cemented—either she would be part of his life or she'd leave for good.

"I'm not sure I want to know," he said.

"Well, I need to tell you." She dropped her hands into her lap. "I love you, Damian. I always have."

CHAPTER FIFTEEN

LAINEY HAD ALWAYS thought the way people described time as standing still after an important moment was a bit of a wank. But now she understood. It was like God himself had planted a hand on the earth to stop its rotation, slowing things down so that each breath dragged into her lungs with agonising slowness.

Damian's expression remained unchanged. His heavy brows crinkled slightly, and the hard set of his jaw was devastating as ever. The lack of reaction was telling.

She'd made a terrible mistake.

"You can't love me." He cringed as soon as the words shot out of his mouth because Lainey jumped, ready to flee. Clearing his throat as if trying to put his thoughts in order, he said, "Stay...please. Let's talk this through."

Oh, God, this was it. The "well, this has been fun but..." talk that she'd always avoided by being the first to cut and run. And now she was going to have to sit and pretend like her heart wasn't shattering into a billion jagged pieces.

Why did you do this to yourself? You know a guy like him will find a picture-perfect wife, not some crazy woman who goes commando and does shooters and dresses up in disguise to seduce men.

Not men. Just him.

"You're panicking." He furled and unfurled his fists, and her hands twitched in response. "I can see it."

"Well, nothing good ever comes after 'we need to talk.' That usually comes before 'I'm not mad, I'm disappointed.'" She tried to muster a smile, but it felt like the bottom had fallen out of her world.

"I worry one of us will be saying that." He frowned. "And it won't be me."

"I know you don't want long term." She couldn't even look him in the eye. "But I thought…"

The weight of his silence pressed down on her heart.

"You're right," he said, eventually. "I *don't* want long term."

Her chest squeezed. "Then maybe we can skip to the part where I leave the country and we forget this ever happened."

Dammit. How pathetic are you? Why don't you drop your heart on the ground so he can stomp on it, already?

"I don't want to forget." His expression was deadly serious. "Lainey, I…fuck, I don't know how to say this."

"Do it. Like a Band-Aid." Her heart stuttered in her chest, tears prickling the backs of her eyes so that she had to blink repeatedly to push them away. "You say, 'Lainey, this has been fun, but you're not the girl for me.'"

He shook his head. "It's not like that."

"Then what *is* it like? Because from where I'm sitting, it looks as though we want different things." She knotted her hands in her lap, praying that the tears would hold off until she was alone.

Alone. It was an idea she had better get used to, because very soon she'd be a whole hemisphere away from her family, her friends. And the man she desperately loved.

"You're supposed to be leaving," he said.

The words were like a bullet ripping her insides to shreds. In his mind, there had always been an end date. She had a ticket and he'd banked on avoiding this conversation. He never had any intention of taking it further.

Did you? You hadn't planned on more than one night. And he wasn't even supposed to know.

But walking away had been so much harder than she'd anticipated. Going back to him without her disguise—being with him as herself—had been everything. The culmination of all her childish, heart-fluttering wishes, of all her lust and desire. Of all her secret dead-of-the-night prayers. And now he'd blown her wide-open. Taken a verbal shotgun to her heart.

"I *am* leaving," she said. "And I shouldn't have come here."

"Lainey, please. Let's not ruin what we had."

"What the hell does that mean?" She stood and

wrapped her arms around herself, taking a step back. But distance wasn't going to save her. Not even when she left Australia. Hell, flying to Mars probably wouldn't help at this point.

She was done. Broken.

Goddammit. Why had she let Corinna and Imogen get into her head? As if he was going to throw up his hands and say "I love you," just like that. But she'd hoped for something…anything. A flicker of feeling. Not the excuse that he thought she was leaving.

He cursed under his breath as he came around the desk. "I don't want to lose you. But that doesn't mean I have anything more to give."

"You have plenty to give, Damian. But you refuse to take the risk." She retreated, taking a step back for every one he took forward. "Or maybe it's that I'm not worth enough for you to try."

Her resigned tone twisted like a blade in his gut. Lainey was the most generous, beautiful, interesting person he knew, and that she felt worthless made him want to rage. His reluctance to enter into a relationship had *nothing* to do with her.

"It's not about that."

"It's probably for the best, anyway," she forged on, her eyes glimmering. "We'd never be equal. I'd end up living in fear, waiting for you to find someone better."

"There isn't anyone better, that's precisely the point." The words came out in a rush—too loud and too close to the bone.

"That doesn't make any sense. Why don't you want to be with me if there's no one better?"

"Lainey, what do you want me to say? I never promised you anything, and there was a bloody good reason for that." He reached for her, but she stepped away so sharply that he froze on the spot. "But that doesn't mean I don't care. I do. So much. *Too* much, which is exactly why I wanted to keep things platonic."

"I never realised how selfish you were," she said. "How self-preserving."

Jenny had looked at him the same way the morning after he'd found her with Ben, when she'd packed her bags to leave for good. Those wide, accusing eyes and that defensive posture that'd screamed *why didn't you try harder?* had frozen him with guilt.

He wanted to fight, but there was nothing left. It would take him some time to process what'd happened—to figure out how to move on. How to repair his relationship with Lainey so that she stayed in the box he needed her to be in—one that wouldn't allow her to get too close.

Walking away now was the smart thing to do— to give them both space to let the heat die down. He had no idea if he could fix things in a way that didn't make her feel rejected.

But he knew one thing for sure: that wasn't going to happen today.

"Self-preservation is important," he said.

"Apparently." Her eyes dragged over him, tears shimmering in a way that made her hazel irises look more green than golden brown. She was so beautiful it was painful to look at her. "Seems like I needed to learn that lesson."

"I didn't want to hurt you." He closed his eyes for a moment, using every ounce of willpower to jam his hands in his pockets so he wouldn't bundle her up in his arms.

"But you did," she said. "I blame me, though, not you."

His head and his heart were at war—one telling him to comfort her and the other telling him to pull the trigger. To end it. He was immobilised by competing tensions—the desire to move forward in opposition with the fear of the past repeating itself.

Words danced on his tongue, so close to tumbling out that he had to hold his breath to keep them in.

I want to be with you.

No. It was guilt and desire talking, and he knew they weren't his allies. He had to stay strong.

"I'm sorry."

"Don't be. You're right, you never promised me anything. I must have heard what I wanted to rather than listening to what you were actually saying." She headed to his door. "I guess I'll see you around... or not."

A second later the door shut with a soft *snick* and Damian stood stock-still, his hands itching to throw something as he listened to her fading footsteps. When the elevator dinged in the outer office, he returned to his chair and slumped down.

He tried to tell himself he'd done the right thing. So why, then, did he feel like the world's biggest bastard?

Damian had a go-to when it came to dealing with problems of the heart: denial. Along with that came an increase in workload so that he didn't have time to think about all the ways he'd fucked up his life. Because there were many. Damian was sure he was successful in his business in spite of himself. In relationships...not so much.

Corinna and Imogen had thrown Lainey a going-away bash the day before, rounding up all her friends and family for a sensational send-off. He hadn't gone. Instead, he'd sat in his suite and pored over the photo that had been waiting for him at the hotel's concierge desk. It was old, slightly discoloured. But he remembered the occasion well. New Year's Day, all those years ago.

She'd left this morning, flying from Melbourne to London via Dubai. According to Google, they'd departed on time and she'd been in the air exactly seven hours and forty-six minutes. He'd set up a notification on his phone so he'd know when she landed.

Why? He had no idea. It wasn't like he was going to call her. What could he possibly say to make things better? Only turning back time could do that. But he had to know that she'd landed safely.

Outside, the sky was vibrant. Below, a festival took place where men dressed as dragons danced along the Southbank boulevard. Their costumes were ruby red, bold and rich. Fierce, like her. His stomach churned in anticipation the way it did every time he thought of Lainey—an uncomfortable mélange of lust, need and regret.

Damian strode onto the balcony and curled his hands around the railing. The area was decorated with a series of fancy potted plants, and he stifled the urge to kick them all over. This itch for destruction would fade…it had to. Because Lainey wasn't coming back, and he wasn't going to change his mind about love. No matter what his dick—or his heart—had to say about it.

A knock on the front door startled him. Who the hell was interrupting his pity party? He hadn't ordered food and had barely eaten a full meal in days. Food wasn't appealing to him right now. He walked inside and grabbed a T-shirt from the back of the sofa, pulling the thin cotton over his head before yanking the door open.

A greeting stalled in his throat when he saw who it was.

"Long time no see." Ben still had the same smarmy grin he remembered. Still wore the same obnoxious red-and-black-striped suit that made him look like a wannabe mobster. Still smelled of too-strong cologne and chewing gum.

"Ben," Damian said flatly. "What the fuck do you want?"

"Is that any way to greet your old mentor?" Ben made a *tsk* sound. "Where are your manners?"

"You weren't my mentor." Damian planted a hand

on the door frame, making it clear that Ben would not be invited in. "And you're not welcome here."

"Can't exactly order me off the property since it's not *your* property, now can you?" His grin widened. "Living in a hotel room is an interesting choice. I know you paid way over market value to get that apartment from Jenny, and yet you're here. Interesting."

He clenched his back teeth, swallowing down the stream of profanity that threatened to erupt. "I've got a new place. Just waiting on the sale to go through."

Lies. But it wasn't any of Ben's business.

"Right." The other man nodded, disbelief painted in his raised eyebrows and cunning smirk. "So, I heard you've managed to seduce one of my clients away from me. I would have come sooner, but it took me a few days to track you down."

Hmm, so clearly Ben hadn't wanted to show his face at Damian's office.

"Not one of your clients, Ben. *The* client." He tilted his chin.

"No, just one client. You see, when you get to where I am, no one client is that important. It's the sum of the portfolio, young grasshopper."

Damian cocked his head. "Your lips are saying one thing, but your eyes are saying something else."

Ben was livid, as predicted. He was trying to act like it didn't matter, like Damian's actions hadn't bothered him in the slightest. But why was he here if he didn't care?

"You can have McPartlin & Co. The old man was

a prick, anyway." Ben shrugged, but the gesture was stiff. "I'm curious, though. What did you say to make him leave? Did you tell him all about how I stole your wife out from under your nose?"

Damian watched his former boss for a minute, letting his loathing roll through him. This man had been his friend once. "I did my job, Ben. I presented him with a plan that will help him save a significant amount of money. Something your people should have already done. If your company was running well, he wouldn't have left."

"You think you're so high and mighty, don't you? The great Damian McKnight, a man of ethics. It's a load of crap. You're no different to me." Ben's jaw ticked. "I thought you were above stooping to our level."

"I'm not fucking someone's wife," he said, coldly. "Don't you dare compare me to you. We're nothing alike."

"You think the fucking is the important bit?" He shook his head. "It's the breach of trust that stings most. You *know* what you're doing is wrong, but you're doing it anyway because you're selfish."

The word was like a slap across his face. Hadn't Lainey said the same thing?

"Hey, don't get me wrong." Ben held up his hands. "I never thought you had it in you. You do have some balls, despite what Jenny has said."

His blood boiled, but he would not let Ben see him lose his shit. The days of wearing his emotions on his sleeve were over. He would *not* be vulnerable in front of this vulture—or anyone like him—ever again.

"Glad to see you and Jenny have been discussing my balls at such length." He yawned. "Was there a reason you came over, or was it just so we could braid each other's hair and shoot the breeze? Because I'm not interested."

"I wanted to hand-deliver this." He pulled a white envelope out of his jacket pocket and handed it over. The front was embossed with Damian's name, and two doves decorated the bottom right corner.

A wedding invitation.

"That's right, we're finally tying the knot. As you well know, it'll be Jenny's second go-around, but there's nothing wrong with a practise run." Ben preened like a ridiculous peacock.

Damian waited for the wave of rage to flow over him, but strangely, it didn't come. It struck him that he didn't give a shit if Jenny and Ben got married because, as far as he was concerned, they deserved one another.

"I wish you a long and happy life together," he said.

Ben blinked. Obviously it wasn't the rise he'd been expecting—or hoping—for. But something Lainey had said had struck him.

If you knew things were going to end anyway, you wouldn't still be pissed about it years later.

It dawned on him that he *had* known things were going to end with Jenny before he caught her with Ben. In fact, he'd thought about how to end their marriage more than once. Naively, he'd assumed she wouldn't want that, despite their numerous arguments. And it wasn't the fact that she'd moved on that'd hurt him. It wasn't even the cheating, now that he thought about it. It was the fact that she'd targeted his boss—someone Damian had once admired and respected—that made him see red.

She'd wanted to hurt him as much as possible.

And how is that different from you specifically targeting Jerry McPartlin? You wanted to hit him where it hurt, too.

Holy shit. Clarity struck him with the force of a head-on collision: by prioritising revenge, by aiming to inflict pain on someone else for his own emotional gain, he'd acted exactly like Ben and Jenny. He'd let what they'd done turn him into the very thing he claimed to hate.

And all the while he'd pushed Lainey away because he was too chicken to put himself in a vulnerable position again. Talk about being a hypocrite.

"I mean it," Damian said. "I hope your marriage is better than what we had. I don't want to wish that on anyone. Not even you."

"Excuse me?" Ben spluttered.

"I won't be attending. But I guess you knew that already." Damian handed the envelope back. "Stop thinking about me and start thinking about your future wife."

He left the other man standing there, shell-shocked, and closed the door. Lainey had been right all along—instead of getting on with his life, he'd been clinging to his own history. Signing Jerry McPartlin hadn't been the key to moving forward—it was simply another rope tying him to his past. A way for him to *feel* like he was making progress, while still trying to protect himself.

But all he'd ended up doing was losing the one woman who saw through all his shit and still wanted him. A woman who was so maddening and intoxicating and wonderful that he should have done everything in his power to make her feel like the goddess she was. He'd failed her. Miserably.

"Not anymore," he said, reaching for his phone. He swiped at the screen and called his assistant, hoping she was still in the office even though he'd left early because he couldn't concentrate.

"McKnight Management, Leila speaking."

Thank God. "Hey. I need you to book me an urgent flight to London. Tomorrow morning."

He grabbed the small suitcase that had his essentials already packed for emergency consulting trips.

"You're meeting with Mr. McPartlin tomorrow," Leila said. Rustling sounded in the background. "Eleven thirty."

"Reschedule it." He hoisted the suitcase onto his bed and flipped it open.

"But it's your first meeting. Mr. McPartlin specifically requested—"

"Reschedule it," Damian repeated. "I need to get to London. His business is running fine. It won't fall apart if he has to wait a few days. And if he can't wait, then he's welcome to leave."

The shocked silence on the other end of the line dragged on for a few minutes before his assistant agreed. Ten minutes later the flight information came through.

Now all he had to do was find out where Lainey was staying and figure out how to make it up to her. It wouldn't be easy, but that was alright. She deserved something honest and real and raw, all the things he'd been afraid of. All the things he knew could hurt him.

But it was time to let go of his safety net. He loved Lainey Kline, and if that made him crazy, then so be it.

CHAPTER SIXTEEN

LAINEY SHIFTED ON the spot, trying to subtly tug at the bodice of her dress. This was the second time she'd stood at a fancy party in a borrowed dress, feeling wholly out of place. Only this time she didn't have a mask to protect her.

"Try to smile, darling," her new boss, Andre, said in his clipped British accent. "There are a lot of important people here."

He wasn't kidding. Though Lainey wasn't up on the who's who of British society, she certainly recognised many of the guests. Vivienne Westwood, Rosie Huntington-Whiteley, Stella McCartney. It was basically a London fashion week party minus the runway show.

"Of course." Lainey nodded and pasted on a smile, but inside it felt like someone had dug her heart out with a spoon.

She'd been in London for only a day and was due to start work on Monday. Her boss was eager to take her out and introduce her to people, and she'd been ready to throw herself into work. She had started helping him pull together some sneak peeks for Instagram stories. But it wasn't giving her the thrill she'd expected or hoped for.

Lainey had worked something out very quickly about Andre Lawrence-Jenkins. His social media strategy was less about building his business and more about making it seem like he lived a charmed life. Lainey would help him see that he needed a more well-rounded approach, but three days in wasn't the time for that conversation. So she dutifully took pictures and made small talk and tried not to wish too hard that she was back in her apartment—wait, no, her *flat*—and tucked up in bed.

"Excuse me a minute." She nodded to her boss, but he barely turned his attention away from the male model who'd come over to chat.

Thankful that she could slip away without argument, she headed toward a courtyard and put on her coat. A few people were smoking by the door, but they hadn't ventured far due to the weather. It was the first time since Lainey landed that the rain had ceased, but it was still bitterly cold. However, air was necessary right now. Between the tight dress and the loud music and the ever-present threat of tears, she needed a moment alone.

Plonking herself down on a wrought iron bench, she shivered as the cold bit through her clothing. This should have been everything she wanted—an exciting new job, an invitation to an exclusive party, opportunities glittering in front of her like city lights. But she was as miserable as the weather. All she wanted was to hear Damian's voice, to feel his lips on hers and the reassuring strength of his chest beneath her cheek.

But he'd rejected her. Confirmed that she would never have what she wanted with him. That her fantasies were stupid and childish, and she'd be forever alone. Or at least destined to continue dating morons because they didn't remind her of him.

She pulled her grandmother's compact out of her clutch and flicked it open. Inside she'd stashed a tiny photo of her with Imogen and Corinna, tucking it into the worn antique frame to keep it secure. The sight of her friends' smiling faces made her heart hurt. She missed them already. She missed her family. And as much as she hated herself for it, she missed Damian, too.

It had been a surprise to learn that homesickness could manifest as actual sickness, and Lainey's stomach had been tied in knots since the second she walked through the security gate at the airport. It was like her body rejected being away from them. People said the feeling would ease over time, but she wasn't sure. Perhaps coming here had been a mistake.

"Is there room on that bench for one more?" A figure loomed over her—dark and imposing. The man wore an immaculate suit with a crisp white shirt and bloodred tie. Covering his face was a black mask.

But they weren't at a masquerade ball.

Lainey shook her head. It couldn't be him. He was supposed to be at home and she was supposed to be here, licking her wounds and trying to figure out how to deal with never having him. Maybe her homesickness had started to cause hallucinations as well as an upset stomach.

She pressed the back of her hand to her forehead. No fever.

"You know this isn't a costume party, right?" she said, frowning.

She stood and wrapped her arms around herself as she moved away from him. But he stopped her with his hand—gentle, yet firm. No one else walked that line like he did.

"Aren't you going to ask my name?" he said. His fingers burned a hole through her coat, his warmth cutting through the layers of wool and cotton.

There was no doubt in her mind. Damian was here. With her. *For* her?

"I don't need to ask." She swallowed. "I know who you are, Rumpelstiltskin."

"Ugly name, isn't it? Curse my parents." His full lips curved to a wicked smile beneath the mask. It made him look even more darkly handsome now that she knew what pleasure and havoc he could wreak on her. "And here I was hoping we'd get to play our guessing game again."

"I'm done with the games."

They were alone in the courtyard, the smokers having retreated as thunder clapped overhead. The rain would arrive any minute, and standing in the open was encouraging danger. But Lainey couldn't move away—she was frozen. Stunned. And still not entirely certain this wasn't a dream.

"So am I," he said.

"Yet you're here, wearing a mask. Why?"

"I needed to see you." His cologne mingled with the heavy air, the scent of impending storm making it feel like she was experiencing him through a veil. It was otherworldly. Dreamlike. "I needed it like I have never needed anything else in all my life."

Her breath stilled. Believing him was hard, because she'd fallen for him over and over again—her heart couldn't take another hit. She was battered and bruised and still in recovery.

"How the hell did you even get in?" She glanced at the doors, which glowed with warm light. "This party is pretty exclusive, in case you didn't know."

His lip twitched. "I have my ways."

"Are you trying to tell me you gate-crashed a party in a mask just to talk to me?"

His soft chuckle rolled over her like a wave, threatening to pull her under and hold her there until the last bit of air was suffocated out of her. "I wish I could say I was as successful a gate-crasher as you, but no. I pulled strings…a lot of them. All of them, actually."

"All of them?" She tilted her face up, terrified of the glimmer of hope in her voice.

"I bribed Imogen and Corinna to find out where you were. I called every person I knew on this side of the world until I found someone who could get me into this party, and I got a call with the lecture of my lifetime from Jerry McPartlin because I bumped his meeting to get on the earliest possible flight." He laughed. "The bastard fired me and went back to Ben."

And he didn't sound the least bit cut up about it. Lainey blinked and shook her head. "But you worked so hard to sign him."

"It was all worth it to see you." His hand came up to tuck a strand of hair behind her ear and she shivered—not from the cold, but from fighting the need to launch herself into his arms. "I love that you kept your hair red. It's perfect on you."

"Damian, stop." She closed her eyes for a second, trying to ground herself. "Why did you do all that?"

"Because you were right. I was chasing revenge and clinging to the past. I wanted to sign him for all the wrong reasons. I would never have pretended to be engaged for any other client, but I was so hell-bent on getting back at Ben that I was willing to do anything."

"Even pretend to be engaged to me," she whispered.

"That part wasn't a hardship, trust me. But it was still wrong."

"And you came all this way to tell me that our fake engagement was wrong." Bitter disappointment clawed at the back of her throat. "Sounds like a waste of a flight."

"I came here to tell you I'm sorry." He cupped her face, brushing at her cheek where an errant tear had fallen. She hadn't even realised her eyes had welled up until she saw the moisture on his thumb when he pulled his hand back. "I shouldn't have involved you in my personal problems. I especially shouldn't have asked you to act for me. But more than that, I'm sorry I was too fucking stupid to acknowledge that you stopped being a friend a long time ago."

"How long?" she whispered.

"Too long. The night you kissed me… God, I wanted to kiss you back. But it wasn't appropriate." He shook his head. "You were so young and vibrant, and I was terrified I was going to drown you with all my baggage."

"Screw being appropriate. I left school the second I could because I was sick of all that *thou shalt behave* bullshit. I won't be forced to fit into someone else's box."

She knew that now. Trying to mask her feelings—whether with a physical mask or with loud clothing and lewd jokes—wasn't working for her. Some of it was real, but much of it was a front. A way for her to pretend like nothing hurt.

But it did. Walking away from Damian that final night had been as painful as any real blow.

"You always danced to the beat of your own drum, didn't you?" he said.

"Yeah. Too bad you wanted some perfect wife who wouldn't buck the rules." She was baiting him. "I can't be that person. I *won't* be that person. I need to be me."

She had to—it was the only way she could be happy.

"You should be you. But I do love that you're crazy enough to dress up in disguise and take what you want." He lowered his forehead to hers. "I love that you don't take no for an answer and you find your own solutions when life doesn't give you what you want."

"Even if I fooled you into sleeping with me?"

"If you hadn't, we probably wouldn't be here now. And I'd still be blind to the fact that I've wanted you for too goddamn long."

"What are you going to do about it?" She squared her shoulders and met his gaze, telling him with her whole body that she wouldn't settle.

The rain fell, drenching them with fat, pelting drops. Her tights clung to her legs, chilling her and making her yearn for the warmth of his lips and hands and tongue. But she wouldn't move an inch until she had what she wanted. Him. All of him. The only man she'd ever loved.

"I'm going to be honest with myself. With you." He gripped her hands, the water running in rivulets over them. "I love you, Lainey Kline. I love your antics, your determination, your loyalty, your incredibly sexy body. I wanted you and I always have, even when I couldn't admit it."

"Why now?" Her voice trembled.

"Because I lost you and it was the single most painful experience of my life." His Adam's apple bobbed. "It felt like someone had ripped my heart out, and I wasn't prepared for it. So I'm here. I gave up McPartlin & Co. and I will give up everything else in my life if it means I can have you. I will move my whole fucking life to this godforsaken storm cloud of a country, if that's what it takes."

The flicker of hope had turned to a blaze, the fire in her heart kindled by his words and his touch. "You'd move here for me?"

"For you, princess, I'd go anywhere."

She threw her arms around his neck and mashed her lips to his. It wasn't a kiss fit for a fairy tale— it was messy and hot. Open and seasoned with rain and tears. The weather continued to bear down, but Lainey wouldn't let go. It was nothing like how she'd dreamed it would be as a girl. But it felt so right. So perfectly imperfect. Like her. Like them.

"I guess I'll have to take you inside now and introduce you around." She grinned. "How are we going to explain the mask?"

"Tell them it's payback." He coaxed her lips apart for another searing kiss. "You fooled me once and now I'm getting you back."

"You're a vengeful man, Rumpelstiltskin." She tugged him toward the light. "You're lucky I love you."

"I am so incredibly lucky." Even with his mask, she could see the sincerity shining in his piercing grey eyes. "And I promise I'll spend the rest of our lives making up for all that time I wasted."

Her eyes darted to the door. "Ah, screw the introductions," she said, pulling him deeper into the shadows of the garden. "Time's a-wasting. Let's start making it up now."

EPILOGUE

Three months later

DAMIAN BOUNCED UP and down on the balls of his feet, jittering like a fighter waiting to swing his first punch. Adrenaline pumped through his veins, turning his usually calm and collected self into a bundle of nerves. Tonight was a big deal. The *biggest* deal.

He *finally* had Lainey back home. All to himself. Her job in London had kept her busy, and she had settled in. Eventually. But doing the long-distance relationship wasn't easy, and she'd insisted he keep his business in Australia. Because she was going to see her six-month contract to completion and then she'd bring all that knowledge home and use it to find her dream job in the place where she belonged. In Melbourne. By his side.

But there was only so much Skype sex that could satisfy him, and with their schedules—not to mention the twenty-four-hour travel time from Melbourne to London—he'd been missing her like crazy. He hadn't seen her in a whole damn month, and it was killing him.

Tonight, however, would be everything he'd been waiting—and planning—for. It'd had taken him a bit longer than he'd wanted to get things arranged. But time had been required to get the stars—or in this case the moon—aligned.

He tapped his foot as he stared at the stream of people in the arrivals area. They all seemed to blend into one human blob, until she appeared. Her bright red hair was a shocking contrast to her all-black outfit. She looked like some kind of sexy superhero ninja.

And it sure as hell felt that way when she launched herself into his arms with all the force her slender frame could manage. He kept his feet firm on the ground and enveloped her, pressing his lips to hers and inhaling the oh-so-familiar scent of her perfume. His hands were in her hair, at her back, holding her so tight because the fear that she would evaporate into thin air was terrifyingly real. His throat felt raw from the emotion rushing up out of nowhere.

Damian wasn't the kind of guy to get all teary, but fuck if he didn't feel a prickle at the back of his eyes. Who the hell was he right now?

"I missed you so much," she said, her own eyes sparkling. "And I really can't wait until they invent teleportation so people don't have to be on a plane for that long."

"Cool your jets, princess. You were in first class. That is nothing to complain about."

She grinned. "I *was* comfortable. But it was way too long before I got to see you."

"You're here now." The words clogged in his throat. "We're together. Everything is right again."

The drive was quick. Lainey filled the car with her chatter and every little update on her life in London, her excitement and happiness radiating out and tangling him up. He'd planned the evening meticulously—every detail was carefully arranged, from the venue to the dessert to the view. And now he found himself as anxious as a teenage boy on his first date.

"So what's your angle tonight?" she asked as he navigated them farther into the city.

"My angle?"

She narrowed her eyes at him. "I feel like you've got something up your sleeve."

He stifled a grin. The sky was darker now, but the city lights were a wash of glitter around them. He pulled up to the building that contained his new home and drove into the underground car park.

"Where are we going?" Lainey peered out of the window, but there wasn't anything to see except concrete pylons and rows of cars. "I thought you said you were staying in the hotel so we could find something when I came back."

"I never said that specifically." He pulled into his parking spot and killed the engine. "Now will you stop it with the questions?"

"Never." She shot him a grin.

How had it happened that he'd fallen head over fucking heels for this crazy girl who was a decade younger than him, who was wild on the surface but loyal and fierce underneath? Who had an open heart and an open mind and a set of legs that totally undid him?

They sat in the car, the silence only broken by the sound of their breath. "Do you trust me?" he asked.

She looked at him with love shining in her face. "Absolutely and completely."

He got out of the car and retrieved her suitcase from the boot. Its wheels squeaked as they walked toward the elevator, and he made a mental note to send her back to London at the end of her week off with a new one.

The second the elevator door opened, Lainey squealed. "I know this elevator!"

"Damn, and I was hoping to keep it a surprise until the big reveal." A roguish smile tugged at his lips and he ran a hand along his jaw.

"When did you move in?" They arrived at the top floor and entered the apartment.

"Last month. They had trouble selling it, so I had the chance to negotiate."

"I know how much you love doing that." She grinned. "I can't believe you bought this place."

The apartment was almost unchanged from when they'd inspected it together, because he wanted her input when she finally returned from London.

"It's perfect," she said, her eyes wide and her hand clamped over her mouth.

"We're going to make it ours, Lainey. Together, as partners." He gently tugged her hand down and scooped her up in his arms. "We're going to decorate it together, and we're going to mark it with memories. When I said I would spend my life making up for lost time, I meant it."

He took her to the bedroom and laid her down on the bed, her red hair fanning out all around her. She looked like a goddess. A vision.

"Don't even think about it," she said, squirming under his grip. "I showered at the lounge on my stopover in Singapore, but that was eight hours ago. You're not getting into my pants yet."

"Don't think about it?" He laughed, crawling up over her body and nudging her legs apart with his knee. "Baby, it's all I'm capable of thinking about. You don't know how hard it makes me to know I've got the woman of my dreams in my bed. *Our* bed. I'm not letting you go until I've felt those beautiful thighs shake around me, until I've heard that sexy, raspy voice begging me to go harder and deeper."

"You think you're so enticing," she teased, looping her arms around his neck. Her back bowed as he pressed his hips down to hers. "And for the record, I know exactly how hard you are."

"It's so good to have you home. Skype doesn't cut it." He pressed his lips to her neck, slipping one hand under her top to find her breast. His cock pulsed, desperate from weeks of knowing nothing but his own hand.

She reached down between them and pulled his zipper down, wrapping her fingers around his cock. "Hmm, home. I like the sound of that."

"Enough talking." He tugged her pants down in one smooth motion.

When he slid into her, it was like everything he'd been waiting for—the feeling of rightness rocketed through him and he bundled her up in his arms the way he'd dreamed of every night since he'd come back home from that first trip to London. Her lips were on his, her body needy and demanding, hips meeting his thrust for thrust as he buried himself inside her. They were still mostly dressed, but he didn't care. Because he needed her now, and not one second could be wasted.

"Lainey," he sighed into her ear as he cradled her, taking and giving with everything he had. "I love you so much."

"I love you, too." Her eyes were heavy-lidded, her cheeks flushed. And the little dent her teeth made in her lower lip was enough to make his entire body shudder with pleasure.

"I'm in this for the long haul, you know." He brushed a strand of red hair from her forehead, touching his lips to hers. "Forever."

"And ever," she whispered, her body trembling as he nipped at her skin. "Just like I always wanted."

* * * * *

LET'S TALK
Romance

For exclusive extracts, competitions
and special offers, find us online:

f facebook.com/millsandboon

@ @millsandboonuk

🐦 @millsandboon

Or get in touch on 0844 844 1351*

For all the latest titles coming soon, visit
millsandboon.co.uk/nextmonth